CROSSING STONES

Also by Helen Frost

Keesha's House
Spinning Through the Universe
The Braid
Diamond Willow

HELEN FROST

CROSSING STONES

4/30/11

For Emily —
Congratulations!
Helen Frost

FRANCES FOSTER BOOKS
Farrar, Straus and Giroux ❖ New York

Library of Congress Cataloging-in-Publication Data
Frost, Helen, date.
    Crossing stones / Helen Frost.— 1st ed.
        p.   cm.
    Summary: In their own voices, four young people, Muriel, Frank, Emma, and Ollie, tell of their
experiences during the first World War, as the boys enlist and are sent overseas, Emma finishes
school, and Muriel fights for peace and women's suffrage.
    ISBN: 978-0-374-31653-2
    [1. Novels in verse.   2. World War, 1914–1918—Fiction.   3. War—Fiction.   4. Soldiers—
Fiction.   5. Friendship—Fiction.   6. Family life—Fiction.   7. Women—Suffrage—Fiction.
8. Michigan—History—20th century—Fiction.]   I. Title.

PZ7.5.F76Cro 2009
[Fic]—dc22

                                                                                          2008020755

Dedicated with love
to my brothers,
Richard and Herb,
in memory of our mother,
Jean Elizabeth Timmons Frost,
1917–2008

CONTENTS

My Mind Meanders Like the Creek

April 1917

My Crooked Mind
Muriel

You'd better straighten out your mind, Young Lady.
    That's what the teacher, Mr. Sander, tells me. As if I could
        stretch the corners of my thoughts like you'd pull
            a rumpled quilt across a bed in an attempt to make
                it look like no one slept there, no one ever
            woke up screaming from a nightmare, or lay there
        sweating till their fever broke, everybody
    scared they'd die—but then they didn't, they got up
and made the bed. My mind sets off at a gallop
    down that twisty road, flashes by "Young Lady,"
        hears the accusation in it—as if it's
            a crime just being young, and "lady"
                is what anyone can see I'll never be
            no matter how I try, and it's obvious
        that I'm not trying. It's history class, which,
    as far as I can tell, they might as well call
war class, all those battlefields, and Generals,
    and Secretaries, capitalized like that—
        not secretaries like Aunt Vera, who
            works for the city of Chicago, and travels
                on her own with money she has saved
            even after she has purchased both the hat
        with three red feathers and the one of deep blue
wool that's lined with silk. No, the Secretaries

whose names we have to memorize for Monday's test
are important people: Secretary of the Treasury,
Secretary of the Interior—in other words,
men. Which is my mistake, to point that out.
*Why is it, Mr. Sander, that in real life
secretaries are always women, but here
in school, all the ones we learn about are men?*
It's a perfectly reasonable question, but everybody
turns to stare, first at me, then at the teacher's blaze of anger:
Miss Jorgensen, are you being smart with me? How
do you answer a question like that? *No, I'm
not,* or *Yes, I am*—either way just gets you
in the same place, only deeper. I try for
middle ground. *Maybe I am,* I say, *maybe
I'm not*—trying to decide what it might mean
to be smart like Aunt Vera and express my own opinions,
compared to what it means when Mr. Sander says it.
I keep on thinking back and forth along
those crooked lines while he is giving me a
talking-to I barely hear until he gets to that
last line—I'd better straighten out my
mind? No thank you, Mister Sir Secretary
Reverend General Your Honor, I think
but do not say. I like the way my mind meanders
like the creek that flows into the northern tip
of Reuben Lake, out the southwest side
into the Little Betsy River, and on and on
from there to who knows where, until
eventually it joins the wild sea.

Our Lives and Our Fortunes
Muriel

We've all heard what is coming: we know
    the president will take us right into the middle
        of this war they're fighting overseas, yet I can't help
            hoping against hope that someone, somehow
                might find a way to keep us out of it.
                Our neighbors, Emma Norman and her parents,
        step carefully across Crabapple Creek on their way
to our house, bringing the newspaper I don't want to see.
Mr. Norman has his usual peppermints for Grace,
    and she, as always, passes them around until there's only one
        left in the bag, then gives the bag to Mrs. Norman—
            Take this home, she says, *and save it*
                for when Frank comes back. She's done that
            at least once a week for the past six months,
        since Frank left for basic training. I have no idea
if Mrs. Norman actually saves them, but the thought is so
big-hearted for a seven-year-old child, maybe Frank
    can taste some kind of sweetness; even all those
        miles away in Kansas, he must know that here
            in Michigan we're missing him. And never more so
                than this evening, as we gather close around the table
            and read the president's address to Congress. *The world*
        must be made safe for democracy . . . To such a task
    we can dedicate our lives and our fortunes,

everything that we are and everything
that we have. He needs *an army of 500,000 men*;
he invokes *the principle of universal liability*
to service. Ollie stands up, puffs out his chest,
and glances across the room at Emma.
Tell me, Mr. President, is my brother
"everything that we are" or is he "everything
that we have"? I only know I'm grateful
he is just sixteen, not old enough
to offer up his everything into your hands.

Apple Trees
Emma

I remember last September, before
Frank left for basic training, he and Ollie
waiting in the apple trees—Ollie on their side
of the creek, and Frank on ours—watching for Muriel
and me to cross Crabapple Creek. Halfway across, where
an eddy spins between two stones, I looked up just in time
to see Ollie throw an apple down at me. I caught it, threw it
back, and to everyone's immense surprise, I somehow hit
Ollie in the arm, which made him lose his balance. I'm
still not sure how he got from tree to water, but there
he was in the creek, spluttering his staunch denial:
I didn't fall, I jumped! Sitting on his backside,
laughing. Tonight I'm remembering that jolly
scene. Muriel, Ollie, Frank, me—us four.

Should We?
Ollie

Sit down and play a tune, Pa suggests.
Should we? In wartime, is it right for us to
make music? Almost half the senior boys, like
Frank and his friends last year, are planning to enlist.
I'd go with them if I could—heck, I'd join up tomorrow
if I thought they'd accept a sixteen-year-old. Could I gain
enough weight, go down to the recruiting office, and try to
bluff my way in by claiming to be eighteen? I bet I'd get a
different reaction from Pa than Ma. Ma would take it in
stride, or try to act like she did. Pa would be furious:
*(Blankety-blank) President Wilson thinks he can just
take away our sons to use for his cannon fodder!*
Would he actually try to stop me, though?
It's likely—so I wouldn't tell him.

Moral Compass
Muriel

Have you raised this girl with no moral compass?
  Mr. Sander questions my parents, then turns
    to me: *If you continue to question our president*
      and the decisions he has made, other students
        may wonder if their classmates are risking
     their lives for nothing. You should be ashamed.
    Mama does hang her head in shame, but I don't, so
  Mr. Sander pushes on: *If we can't stand together*
as a free country, what are our boys fighting for? At that,
  Papa looks straight into Mr. Sander's eyes. He doesn't say
    what he sees (the eyes of a coward?), because Papa is kind,
      thoughtful about others' feelings. *I know my daughter*
        is opinionated, he says, *but there is no law*
     against that. (*So far,* he mutters under his breath.)
    Muriel has every right to speak her mind.
  Mr. Sander withers under Papa's steady gaze, and we
go home. Papa drives the horses gently; we ride in silence
  for a mile or so, and then he says, *You're graduating soon;*
    don't worry too much about what Mr. Sander thinks—
      but there are others like him in this world.
        Be a little careful of such people, Muriel.
    "A little careful"—maybe—but then Mama adds,
You may need to learn to bite your tongue.
Is that what women—"ladies"—are supposed to do?

9

Bite off little pieces of ourselves,
     our very thoughts? Chew on them
         until they don't seem so worthwhile—
            and then what? Swallow them? Or spit them out
               and crush them underfoot, until we can
            be absolutely sure no one will know
         they ever crossed our minds!

Fragrance of Lilacs, Sweet Scent of Skunk

May 1917

Deep Quiet
Emma

Such good solid stuff
Ollie is made of—these words
declaring war are playing on his mind.
When anything "must be made safe," Frank
and Ollie always volunteer. Now, with Frank's life
on the line, Ollie tries to help my family. Our fence has
been broken for a month; no doubt he started fixing it today
because it keeps his hands occupied as he tries to find a way
to think about what this war will mean, for all of us. He's as
quiet as the fence itself: measure the wire, open the knife,
cut the wire, close the knife, quick twist, hard yank—
yes, the fence will hold. Above us, the kind
of sky that greets a thousand bluebirds.
So sweet a day. So tough.

Socks
   Muriel

Thirty-seven years ago in Denmark,
   two sisters married two brothers. It's
         like an anthem, the way Papa tells it: *To*
               this day, your Danish relatives would claim you
                     if you walked into the old family home.
         But when Mama tells the story, she's seeing
         Ollie with the Normans' daughter, Emma—
and me with Emma's older brother, Frank,
pairing us up like she rolls up pairs of socks,
      that little sigh of satisfaction when they come out even—
         or "close enough," if there's one black sock,
               one navy blue, left over at the end.
                     Emma is my closest friend; Frank and Ollie
                     are like brothers. Mrs. Norman comes here
            with her sewing almost every afternoon,
      or Mother goes to their house—they seem to think
they know us better than we know ourselves.
      But I don't see myself going down the road they
            see me on, leading to a clean white farmhouse
                  not too far from here, me out in the yard, my
                     apron pockets full of corn I'm scattering
                  for biddy hens. I love Emma like a sister, and
         I'm as scared as anyone that Frank will be
sent overseas to fight this war—I'm delighted

that he's coming home on leave next week—
        but slow down, Mother: I have no
                intention of becoming the Mrs. Norman of your
                        imaginary future. Who I am remains to be seen—
                and I alone intend to be the one to see it.

Lightning
Ollie

Gray sky, all-day rain,
thunder coming closer. Lightning
struck the barn in just this kind of storm
last summer. It took us the entire fall and winter
to rebuild the part of the hayloft that burned in the fire
that night. Our work is sound—Pa and I work well together,
though I wonder: Will he do as well without me? *Ollie, let me
show you something!* Grace runs up. I've told her we can use the
scrap wood for a playhouse; now she's found a place to build it.
You said you would, Ollie. Come on—look! If I work hard and
fast I might get it done in my spare time. (Maybe, with
luck, I'll build up my muscle and look older.) I sort the
lumber. *I might not finish it before . . .* I start to
say. *Before what, Ollie?* I don't answer.

Ten Days Home
Muriel

Frank has finished his training; now
    he has ten days of home leave. Then—
        nobody can say for sure, but it looks like
            he'll be shipped overseas. We meet him
                at the station—I'm the first to see him (I can't
            help noticing how his shoulders fill his uniform),
        but I stand back when three girls surround him
    as he jumps from the train, swinging his duffel bag
across his back. He scans the crowd—his eyes light on us
    (on me?) as Grace sees him and runs to hug him.
        He lifts her in the air and swings her high (she
            almost kicks Edith Morgan in the jaw),
                and Frank is ours for these few days.
        We all gather at the Normans' house for dinner—
    Mrs. Norman slices a clove-studded ham; Emma's baked
a batch of "Grandma Jean's Best Dinner Rolls";
Mama and I made a four-layer devil's food cake;
    and after Frank has eaten three large pieces, he plays
        a few tunes on his banjo, Papa plays his fiddle,
            and we sing until long after dark. Mama
                lets Grace stay up an hour past her bedtime—
        Frank shows her how to pluck a few notes
    of "It's a Long Way to Tipperary,"
and teaches her six verses, nodding to her

when he sings "to the sweetest girl I know."
 Grace smiles up at him—she may just be
 the sweetest girl any of us will ever know.
 I breathe in this all-together of our life—
 how can there be war in a world where
 Ollie's baritone and Emma's alto
 harmonize so perfectly?

Why Not?
Muriel

Frank's home leave threatens to eclipse
    my graduation, until he asks if I'm going
        to my graduation dance with anyone—
            Well, no—and, if I'd like him to take me.
                I'm so surprised, I almost ask the question
            that pops into my mind: *Was this your mother's*
        idea, Frank, or yours? I stop myself because
he stutters as he asks me—*M-M-Muriel,*
shifting from one foot to the other—Frank
    who is always so confident and full of fun.
        I can't help smiling as I answer: *Yes, I'd like that.*
            He stops stuttering, grins, and says, *Our mothers*
                will be happy. Exactly what I'm thinking.
        A little too happy for my taste, I say.
        Frank shrugs. *Who says we have to tell them?*
We agree—we don't! As I'm sewing my dress
(blue satin that swirls around me when I walk), I refer to it
    as my graduation dress. And when Mama asks me
        if I'm going to the dance, I simply say, as she
            so often does, *We'll see, when the time comes.*

A Greater Good
Muriel

I should have been the valedictorian. *Does it bother you,*
    Emma asked me, *to be smarter than all the boys?*
        No, it doesn't bother me, but Mr. Sander couldn't stand
            to hear me give a speech—who knows what radical ideas
                I might express. He gave me a D in comportment
                (Comportment: Who I am! How I conduct myself!)
      so my final average fell one quarter point below
    Arthur Anderson's, and now we are listening
to Arthur lecture us: *We must all Put Others First*
in this Time of our Country's Greatest Need.
    We must Sacrifice our Selfish Dreams
        for a Greater Good. The teachers and parents
            and half the students get out their handkerchiefs
        to dab tears from their eyes, and call attention to
      their sniffles. Silently, I argue against every word
    that Arthur says: If we do put others first, if we love
the ones we love and trust people everywhere
    to do the same, wouldn't we stop sacrificing one another,
        fooling ourselves into believing that such sacrifice would solve
            our problems? Wouldn't we be free to pursue
          those selfish dreams that might, if
      everyone is putting others first,
    lead to a genuinely greater good?
I'm still steaming about all this

when Frank offers me his arm to walk
from the school to the dance hall. The soft swish
of my dress doesn't stop me from stomping along,
arguing point by point with Arthur's speech.
Why is everyone just doing what they're told?
The presidents of all the countries should
meet somewhere and fight this war themselves
if they think it's worth fighting.
What are they *sacrificing? Have they asked the mothers*
who gave the best years of their lives to raise
these boys the presidents are sending into battle?
No! Women don't even get to vote—it isn't fair!
Frank listens for a while, then says, *You're starting*
to sound like one of those Woman Suffragists, Muriel.
It doesn't sound very patriotic. But who cares?
You graduated! Let's dance! And so we do,
together, and with other friends—I dance with all
the boys except for Arthur, who doesn't ask me,
and Frank dances with each of the twelve girls
in my class, and then he and I dance
the last dance, relaxing into each other's arms,
Frank's heartbeat steady in my ear. I have to admit,
I'm enjoying this, and when the dance is over,
it's nice to walk outside into the night,
with Frank, my almost-but-not-quite brother.

Someone
    Muriel

The horses clip-clop down the road ahead of us—
        the fragrance of lilacs, then the sweet scent of skunk,
            a chorus of crickets and spring peepers. It's not often
                Frank and I are alone together, neither Emma
                    nor Ollie with us. Frank clears his throat.
                    Did you know, Muriel, that Ed and Howard
                enlisted yesterday? I say nothing. He goes on.
        John and Hal are planning to sign up next week. It's dark—
Frank can't see me roll my eyes. *The ants go marching . . .*
        is my only comment. That childish song is still
            singing itself in my head as we come home
                and Frank holds out his hand to help me
                    from the buggy, as if I were a fine lady,
                and he Sir Galahad. And then: *May I*
            kiss you, Muriel? So gently asked,
        a sweet surprise. A kiss would change
so much—I hesitate. *Ordinarily,* he says, *I wouldn't be*
in such a hurry; you know me, I always take my time.
        But—I've been trying to tell you—
            I'm going to France. I leave next Monday.
                It would sure be nice to have a girl
                back home to write to—someone waiting
        for me, someone to keep fighting for.
A girl. Someone. He doesn't have time

to choose, to court, to fall in love,
and here I stand. It must seem easy, obvious.
But— *No, Frank,* I answer, *I can't*
do that for you. I'll be glad to write to you;
you know we all will. Grace will keep on
sending you her little drawings. We'll miss you—
I'll miss you—more than I can say.
I wish you wouldn't go. I wish no one would . . .
Frank shakes his head. Am I confusing him?
Has he planned how this should work—get a girl,
go to war, come home a hero, and get married?
His smile fades—if I believed that one sweet kiss
could bring it back, I might
want to give him that small comfort.
But no. Frank signed up for this.
I didn't. It is not up to me
to make it easier.

Would It Hurt?
Emma

A kiss is not a marriage vow,
I argue with Muriel. *For pity's sake,*
would it hurt you to give Frank a little dream
to tuck into his heart before he leaves? One kiss—
you wouldn't be engaged, just something for my brother
to hang on to in the lonely times when he's far from home.
I don't know exactly what happened between you last night,
but from Frank's face today, it's not hard to guess. He might
not come back from this war! Are your ideas so set in stone
that you can't put them aside, or at least consider another,
more gentle point of view? Believe me, Muriel, I hate this
war as much as you do, but truly, in the overall scheme
of things, would one little kiss be so hard to take?
Muriel's only answer is, *I don't know.*

Right in Front of Everyone
Ollie

Light in the eastern sky has turned
from red to gold in the hour we've been
standing here with Frank, waiting for the train
to take him back to camp. Emma looks at her brother
as if she thinks he's already been to war and is returning
home a few feet taller, covered in ribbons and medals. She
stands on tiptoe and kisses him on the cheek, then folds her
hands around his arm. (For a look like that from Emma, I'd
roam the earth, swim across oceans and fight lions.) Muriel
has not yet said goodbye. Looking up at Frank, she says,
You don't always have to be the hero. You stay safe now!
Commanding him with such ferocity that he jokes,
Come here and say that. And when she does,
right in front of everyone, he kisses her!

Circles for the Crossing Stones

June 1917

Would You Be Willing?
Muriel

Look, Mama—Papa forgot his lunch—
Ollie's over at the Normans', helping
with the planting—I'll hitch up the horses
and take this to Papa at the lumberyard.
It's good to be out on this warm day,
half an hour into town, and half an hour back,
time to think my own thoughts, sing to the horses,
wave to men out in the fields—though lately
half the people in the fields are women,
and at the lumberyard, six women, wearing overalls,
are working just as hard as men. *They're filling in*
for men who have been drafted, Papa tells me.
All the way home, and all afternoon, I think about
applying for a job myself—I'd earn some money, and
it's considered "the patriotic thing to do" these days.
But at supper, Mama tells us *she* has decided to go to work
at a shop in town. The bookkeeper was drafted,
and the manager asked Mama to help out
"for the duration"—that's the phrase they're using, to avoid
having to say "war." (No one knows, of course, how long
the duration will be.) *Muriel, would you be willing*
to take care of Grace and help with the housework?
"Help with the housework"—ironing and mending,
washing dishes, cooking, milking, churning, mopping.

And, oh yes, "take care of Grace," as if that's
    a little thing you do when all the other work
        is finished. Mama and I together are barely
            keeping up with everything; I don't see how
                I'll do it all myself. But this is not a question.
            It's a request that will define my days—
        for the duration. Grace shines a little grin
    my way when Mama turns her back—
no doubt thinking of some mischief
    I'll allow that Mama wouldn't.

The Gentleman Should Always
Muriel

Grace draws a picture: our two houses with the creek
    between them, circles for the crossing stones
        spaced across the creek, stick-people
            standing on the circles holding hands,
                a small girl with brown braids (Grace)
            between two bigger girls—she means them to be
    straight-haired Emma and curly-haired me—
and a slightly taller boy—obviously Ollie—
holding Emma's other hand. On my other side,
    she's drawn a stone with no one on it, my hand
        stretched out toward it, reaching out to someone
            who's not there. *I drew this for Frank,* she says.
                Can we send it to him? I've been thinking
            I could write to him—why not? *Yes, Grace,*
    let's do that, I say. *I'll write a note to send him,*
along with your picture. Frank will enjoy that.
It's harder than I thought to find the words I need:
Dear Frank, How are you? ~~I'm~~ (no . . .)
    We're guessing you're in France by now.
        There's a lot of work to do around here—
            you know how it is this time of year—
        picking the strawberries, weeding the beans.
    Boring. I tear it up. I'm looking out the window,
chewing on my pen, when Mama comes home

from her new job. *Muriel, are you writing to Frank?* she asks.
I bend my head over the paper, but I can't hide
the blush that rises—*Oh,* I mumble,
Grace drew a picture, I'm only . . .
I'm not aware I know this rule, until
I'm embarrassed to be caught breaking it:
*The gentleman should always
be the first to write,* Mama informs me.
A lady never writes until she has received a letter.
Grace bursts into tears. *I drew this for Frank!*
Why can't I send it? Mama smiles down at her.
*Don't be silly, Grace. You're a little girl,
not a young lady. I'll help you mail your drawing.*
The two of them go in the other room to find
an envelope, and I pick up my pen and try again
to find the words I want to say to *My dear Frank . . .*
No. *Hello, my friend?* No . . .

Frank's Absence
Emma

Summer is different now. Bessie demands
we clean her stall; Frank isn't here, so it's up to me.
Who will help Father plow the field? *Ollie will help,* I say—
yes, here he comes now, whistling through our door just as I stoke
the fire to heat some soup for lunch. But even Ollie can't fill the empty spot
that Frank leaves, an odd-shaped missing piece in the jigsaw puzzle of our lives.
And maybe worse—what I did not expect—although we all claim nothing can fill
that space, somehow the chores *do* get done. Mother takes the wheat to the mill;
I watch Grace while Muriel helps Father shoe the horses. We sharpen knives;
we pitch the hay. Mother and I help Father birth the calf—Bessie does not
even seem to realize Frank isn't here. Muriel's father makes a joke
to mine about turning us into boys while Frank is away.
Even as we figure out who will do what, we
hold his place open, however we can.

Rocking
Muriel

The hand that rocks the cradle is the hand that
    rules the world, Mama says, by which she means
        I should be content to learn the women's work
            that she and Mrs. Norman do so smoothly
                anyone would think there's nothing to it—
            until a day like today when I almost burn
        the house down making eleven pints
    of strawberry jam—how should I know
paraffin can catch fire so easily?
        I ignore my burning hand and rush to the creek
            for a bucket of cold water—only to discover that water
                fans the flames instead of putting out this kind of fire.
                    I'm never going to get married! Never! I burst out.
            Mama tries to quiet me: *No one's talking*
        about marriage. Calm down, Muriel—all's well
    that ends well. It's a good thing it happened
on a Saturday when I'm at home. She thinks
    I can be soothed and smothered,
        like the fire she extinguishes so quickly,
            so competently, it doesn't even burn the blanket
                she puts over it—where did Mama learn to do that?
        She smiles her sweetest, most infuriating smile
    as she wraps a bandage around my blistered hand.
Women influence the world in quiet ways,

she says. *We keep peace in our families, and*
    raise our children to be decent, honest people.
        Decent. Honest. (Frank)
            But what good does that do, I argue, *if your*
                decent, honest children are sent off to fight
            and maybe die in a war someone else
        started, and all the girls and mothers
    in America have no way of stopping?
She holds my bandaged hand, pushes
    a strand of hair from my flushed face.
        I don't know the answer to that question,
            she finally admits. She studies me:
                Maybe you won't rock a cradle, Muriel.
                Some women seem to prefer to rock the boat.
    She speaks gently, thoughtfully; there's truth
    in what she sees and says. But her words sting
like yellow jackets flying from a nest I don't
    know is there until I step right into it.

Geranium
Ollie

Will Emma write to me? I can't ask
because I'm not saying goodbye to anyone.
They'll all know, by this time tomorrow, that I've
left home to catch the train to Kansas for basic training.
What will Pa do when he finds out I enlisted, underage? I
think it's better not to tell him. Grace asks, *Why are you
being so nice to me now, Ollie?* I've been spending all my
free time finishing her playhouse. Emma hung new
pink curtains in the windows. Now she holds the
cat in her lap, stroking it. This morning, Grace
slept on an old quilt as I pounded in one last
nail and looked around. *Remember this:*
Emma's hand on the freshly painted
sill as she waters a red geranium.

Your Son and Brother
  Muriel

We wake up and Ollie's not here—nothing
        so unusual; he's probably gone over to the Normans'.
                Mama and Papa go to work, I milk Rosie
                        and make breakfast, Grace wakes up and eats it.
                        I feed the chickens, churn the butter.
                It's early afternoon when Mrs. Norman
        comes to ask if Ollie might spare an hour or so
to help them fix a leak in their roof. *What?*
I thought he'd been at your house since
        six o'clock this morning. We look everywhere
                in both our houses, anyplace he might be working.
                        Grace says, *He finished my playhouse yesterday.*
                                Emma made pink curtains! We look there.
                No. And then the mailman comes,
        with Ollie's letter: *You'll receive this*
on Wednesday afternoon, after I have left.
I'm headed to Kansas for basic training.
        You might think I'm too young, but I'm
                only twenty months younger than Frank. It's been
                        rough on me, thinking of him over there while I
                                stay safe at home. I had no trouble getting
                        the recruiters to believe I'm eighteen—
                think of it this way: by the next time you see me,
I will be. Pa, don't go in and try to change this—

if they find out my real age, it could cause trouble.

I'll write again when I get settled in.

Ma and Muriel, I know you would have made me

a chicken dinner if you'd known I was leaving,

but I hope you'll understand why I decided

not to tell you. I'll look forward to that

dinner when I get home. Don't be sore.

Your son and brother, Ollie.

The Normans come over and we all talk

through supper, and on and on until the sun goes down.

Papa wants to follow Ollie on tomorrow's train.

I'll go in his place, if they'll let me.

He's a mere boy. I'm not too old.

But Mr. Norman convinces Papa

that Ollie is right: *A dishonorable discharge*

for lying about his age could follow him

all through his life. Mama and Emma keep talking

about the danger he'll be in. It scares me, too,

but for once I keep my opinions to myself.

If I start talking, I'm afraid I might admit

how my thoughts keep turning from the war

to Ollie's chores. Who will do them now?

Conversation Through a Thick Curtain

July 1917

Love to Everyone
Muriel

Emma comes leaping over the crossing stones,
    waving a letter: *It's from Frank! He's in France now.*
        He says the trip over was terrible, everyone was seasick,
            but now they're getting ready to fight. He sounds
                excited, he sounds proud—here, read it yourself.
            I take the letter from her and turn away
        so she can't see my hand trembling,
    heaven knows why—it's not as if Frank
is *my* brother, it's not as if . . . Well, in any case,
    I'm glad to know he has safely crossed the ocean:
        The sea voyage was very rough, but at least
            we finally got some time to write a few letters,
                and tomorrow we'll be able to mail them.
        The food is terrible—Mother, what I'd give
        for a dish of your apple crisp, warm from the oven.
    But I can't complain—the blisters on my heels
have turned to calluses, and I guess we're all
    as ready as we'll ever be for what comes next.
        Tell Ollie thanks for helping on the farm.
            ~~*Tell Muriel*~~— Why has he crossed that out?
        My love to everyone, Frank.

2:25

    Muriel

One good thing about Mama's working:
    I'm the one to meet the mailman
        at 2:25 this afternoon while Grace
            is taking her nap. *Dear Muriel, Thank you*
                for your letter. I meant to apologize
                for my behavior on the train platform.
        I'm glad to see you aren't holding that
    against me. I don't know what came over me—
you looked so pretty in that yellow blouse, I guess
    I got carried away. Well, we're in France now,
        and I'm afraid there's not too much to write about,
            unless you're interested in trench shovels,
                mud, the sound of other fellows snoring
            all night long. You're not? I didn't think so.
        How's everyone at home? Tell Grace
    I liked her picture, and she can draw me
standing with the rest of you on that last stone. That's
    where I see myself whenever they give us time
        to think of home. Which isn't often.
            Yours, Frank.

Seeing Things
Emma

Everywhere, I'm seeing
things that make me think of
Ollie. The red geranium in Grace's
playhouse window—his last day, when
he knew he'd be leaving, but I did not. A hay
bale's wisps of hay stick out like Ollie's hair—I
reach out to tuck them back into his hat. The cat,
lost for three days, comes home skinny—even that
makes me wonder: Is Ollie eating well? When a fly
lands on my arm, I remember Ollie's arm, the way
he'd flex his muscle, showing off. The white hen
is laying three or four eggs every day in places
she never has before: Wouldn't Ollie love
an omelet? (He is only sixteen!)

Careful
Muriel

Papa slaps the newspaper down on the table.
  They've gone and done it. Now it is, in fact,
      against the law for Muriel to speak her mind
          as freely as she'd like. I read the article:
              Congress has passed an abominable law,
          the Espionage Act, which threatens punishment—
      twenty years in prison! a ten-thousand-dollar fine!—
  for arguing against the war. It's now illegal
to mail newspapers, or even letters, that give arguments
      against the draft. *Does this mean Aunt Vera can't write to us*
          like she always does, telling us about her suffrage
              meetings and why she and her friends are angry
                  about the war, especially the draft—remember
              that article that called it "a new kind of slavery"?
      Papa paces, door to table, table back to door.
  I don't know, he says. *They're not likely to arrest my sister,*
but the worst of this is—this! Exactly what is happening
right here in this room, right now. Mama
          doesn't see it the way we do. She listens and then
              puts in her two cents' worth: *Be careful, Muriel,*
                  in what you write to Frank. I glance at her—
              how does she even know about our letters?
      Most likely from the nosy postmistress
  who sorts the mail and shares our party line;

I bet she listens in on my private conversations
     and tells my parents things she's heard me say
          to Emma. As for Mama's admonition
               to be careful, I have to smile—the letters
                    Frank and I exchange could hardly
          be more careful than they are.

Adventure
  Muriel

Frank writes letters to Emma and his parents—
    Emma shows them to me—cheerful,
        hearty: he's having an adventure
            he can't wait to tell them all about
                when he gets home. He's met people
                from all over the world! Soldiers from India
            who don't use helmets—they wrap their heads
    in turbans! Scottish soldiers who wear kilts
that look like skirts. Frank hopes to visit
    Scotland when he gets a few weeks'
        leave, probably three months from now.
            How are the crops? Is everyone well?
                He's proud to serve his country.
                Don't worry about him, he's doing just fine.

Frank Writes to Me
Muriel

I'm surprised they even sent this letter,
    after censoring so much of it. I read what I can,
        then hold it up to the light and guess the rest.
          Frank must have written something
             other than what he knows he is allowed
          to say, but now he'll think he's told me
        things I haven't read—it's frustrating, like trying
    to carry on a conversation through a thick curtain.
Dear Muriel, Thank you for writing to me.
    I bet it's hard on you, trying to keep up
        with all the work. (Did I complain too much?)
          Don't go burning down the house, now.
            I'm glad you don't sugarcoat things
          when you write to me, Muriel—
        I'll try to do the same, ~~though as you know,~~
~~all our letters have to pass through censors,~~
~~so I can't tell you everything. To tell the truth,~~
    ~~it's a mess over here, and~~ *no one can say*
        when this war might be over. ~~Death smells like~~
          ~~rotten fish~~ (Is that word "fish"? He went fishing?),
          ~~and sounds like a rabbit with its foot caught in a trap.~~
          ~~I hate to tell you all this, Muriel. I want you to~~
        think of me laughing, on a Sunday picnic
      with you and Ollie, Emma, and little Grace—

I was surprised, when I was home, to see how tall she was!
If you tell me about your days there, and I
tell you about mine over here, we'll know
each other better by the time I get home.
(I would like that.) *I think of you more*
than I should, I suppose. (How much
should we think about each other?)
~~*I'm beginning to wonder if you might be right*~~
~~*in some of your opinions*~~—*that's all I'll say.*
You'll know what I mean. From your good friend, Frank.
P.S. Tell Ollie ~~NOT *to sign up for this unless*~~
~~*they draft him and he can't get out of it.*~~
("NOT"? "drift"? or "draft"? I can't make it out.)
I'll do my best to get the job finished
before he's old enough to join me here.
I don't show Frank's letter to anyone.
I spend long hours weeding the garden,
picking peas and thinning rows of beans,
letting my mind go where it will—which is,
most often, straight to Frank and Ollie:
What makes boys go to war? Did Ollie sign up
because Frank did, or does he honestly believe
the president is right? If those speeches about democracy
are true, why do they censor the soldiers' letters home?
Let our boys write and tell us what they know.
Let us write back and tell them what we think.

Blisters
Ollie

Latrine digger, message boy,
pot scrubber—not exactly my idea of
life as a soldier. Almost everyone at this training
camp is faster and stronger than I am—they're all older
by several years. I can't get out of this. I should have waited
two and a half years, until I am nineteen—except by then, Frank
could be home. (Will I see him over there?) By that time, maybe I
would have missed the whole war. Okay. Don't think about home.
Too late now to go back. Time to lace up my boots, strap on
my pack, and move out into formation. My socks are
damp and muddy. Bloody blisters on both heels.
Right, LEFT, right . . . Could I kill a man?
(Not *man*. Enemy: *Enemy Soldier*.)
What if Muriel is right?

Courage
   Muriel

I try not to look as if I'm waiting, but it must
        be obvious: here comes the mailman, smiling—
            A letter for you, Miss Jorgensen, and one
                    for your parents. One from Frank for me?
                        Ollie's for all of us? I'm right about Ollie—
                but as it's not addressed to me, I put it aside.
            My letter . . . is not from Frank. Familiar
        handwriting I can't quite place—Aunt Vera?
Why would she write to me, rather than to Papa?
        Dear Muriel (small, careful script), *I'm writing*
                to you because I'm about to embark on a journey
                    some might consider foolhardy, and many
                            are suggesting could be dangerous.
                    I sent your family, as I always do, the most recent
                issue of Suffrage News, *but it was returned—*
        the post office will no longer deliver what the government
deems unpatriotic. (Come to think of it, it is a long time
    since we've heard from Aunt Vera—no letters,
            no newspaper clippings, no political cartoons
                    from the Chicago papers.) *It is not right that women*
                        should have no voice in these matters of great
                    concern to us. President Wilson has his mind
            on the war at the moment, but I, and many others,
    refuse to let him ignore our cause—universal

suffrage for all adult citizens, in all states.

    I am going to Washington to join the picket line
        in front of the White House. (Have you heard
            any news about this?) I am writing to say
                I am doing this for you, Muriel, and for
            Grace—for all the girls yet to be born. I expect
        to be in Washington for one week. I'll stop to see you
    on my way home so that I can speak to you in person
about the reasons for what we are doing.

    You give me courage, my dear Muriel.

    I look forward to seeing you soon.

        With love, Aunt Vera. I read the letter
            over and over—foolhardy? dangerous?
        She says I give her courage—how
    can I give what I don't have myself?

Fifteen Words
Muriel

Dear Ma and Pa,
    I'm fine. Could you send me some socks?
      Your son, Ollie.
          Papa pores over the Sears catalog
             as if he's ordering a tractor.
       What do you think, cotton or wool?
      What size? How many pairs?
Mama spends the weekend furiously
knitting—and finishes two pairs of socks by
    Monday morning. I bake oatmeal macaroons
      and Grace draws a detailed portrait of the cows
        to add to the parcel we send off to Ollie.
          No one says what we're all thinking:
        fifteen words after three weeks does not
     sound "fine." Could I board tomorrow morning's
train—to Chicago, and from there to Kansas—
and take these socks and macaroons to him myself?
    If, as I suspect, Ollie is not fine, could I tell
      someone he's too young to go to war?
        Could I bring my brother home?

Politics
Emma

I've never really understood
why Muriel gets herself so involved
in politics. I don't know why she'd *want*
to vote. When I look at all the things women
have to think about already—cooking, mending,
laundry, gardening, babies, keeping house—I don't
know when we'd find time to decide who'd be the best
man (or maybe woman!) for president, and for all the rest
of the government. Voting and expressing myself won't
change anything. Will it keep the army from sending
Ollie overseas? Will it bring Frank back home any
sooner? And what if I'm wrong? I simply can't
be as sure of myself as Muriel, so resolved,
so certain of what's right and good.

A Long, Low Moooooooo
Ollie

Guess they got my letter. It's great,
getting this package from home the day before
we leave. New socks (clean and dry!); oatmeal cookies;
long letter from Ma, Pa, and Muriel; one from Emma; and
a picture from Grace—I think it's Rosie and her new calf. She
drew a big smile on Rosie's spotted cow-face—I could swear I
heard a long, low *moooooooo* when I unfolded the paper, and it
occurred to me: if I tuck it into a pocket of my knapsack, with a
few of Muriel's macaroons, it will be like a window to home. I
may run into Frank over there—he'd love to see these things.
Strong as all this hard training has made me, I still feel like
me—and I'm afraid that's not saying much. The sun is
setting on our last day in America. Am I up to the
test I'm about to face? I don't know.

Like a Rain-Soaked Wool Jacket

August 1917

"Kaiser Wilson"
Muriel

I'm not sure we should let Muriel read it,
      Mama says to Papa as I walk in the door.
            After milking Rosie, feeding the chickens,
                  and helping Grace find a dozen eggs,
                        then bandaging a cut she got on her knee
                  when she fell off her swing onto a piece
            of broken glass—suddenly, now, I'm a child?
      What is it they're not sure I should read? Papa
answers me before I ask: *It's a hard letter*
      we've received from Aunt Vera, Muriel. She
            was injured as she held a banner in front
                  of the White House. Mama purses her lips.
                    If you're going to tell her, tell her what
                  the banner said. I already know. I saw it
            in the newspaper, although I didn't know
      Aunt Vera had been holding it.
The paper called it the "Kaiser Wilson
      banner," accusing President Wilson of being
            like the Germans we're fighting in the war.
                  HAVE YOU FORGOTTEN YOUR SYMPATHY
                        WITH THE POOR GERMANS BECAUSE THEY
                WERE NOT SELF-GOVERNED? the banner asks,
            then declares, for the president to read
            every day when he walks by: 20,000,000

AMERICAN WOMEN ARE NOT SELF-GOVERNED.
It goes further than they've gone before,
true, but they have a point. Mama is outraged:
What do they expect? It's a slap in the face
to all our boys and everything we're fighting
for. Ollie, her own nephew, is on his way
to fight the Germans—those women are undermining
him, and Frank, and all our boys. It isn't right.
If you ask me, she says (though no one has), *Vera*
should expect exactly this, and worse. She looks at me,
daring me to disagree. I hold out my hand to Papa
for the letter. *How badly was she injured?*
He gives it to me. *Not badly enough to keep her*
off the picket line long enough to stay out of prison.
Now she's been arrested. I read the scribbled note
on the outside of the envelope: "I'm giving this
to Ruby Madsen, to mail to you. I don't expect
I'll be writing any letters for a few weeks."

Bluebird
Emma

Saturday afternoon. A bluebird
flies against our kitchen window. Mother
says, *Keep that window closed! Don't let it in.*
When I go out to look beneath the window, I find
the bird on the ground, stunned but warm, still living.
I hold it in my hands and sing a lullaby, some psalms,
and other songs I know by heart, until its wings spread
against my hands, and it flies. I go on kneading bread,
the bluebird's heartbeat in my fingertips, my palms.
This evening, slicing into the fresh loaf, I'm giving
some to Father (pumpernickel, his favorite kind)
when a warm breeze moves across my skin.
Look: the bluebird, on the screen. Neither
Mother nor I breathe, or say a word.

In the Night, Through Towns
Ollie

Dread weighs me down
like a rain-soaked wool jacket.
We move in the night, through towns
where little girls like Grace must be asleep
in their warm beds, through countryside where
cats toss mice around in dark corners of the barns.
One thing bothers me: I don't know the overall plan.
None of us do. They're moving us to the battlefront,
that's obvious. I'm sure they have a strategy for us to
win; maybe they'll fill us in. To tell the truth, I don't
care as much about their lofty goals as I do about
seeing my family again—there's a man on a
bike, pedaling into morning, bringing
bread home to his family, I bet.

A Few Eggs, Five Peaches, All the Peas

September 1917

Restless
Muriel

I'm glad not to be going to school this year—no more
        homework, no more Mr. Sander, no more poetry
            to memorize or history to learn or essays to
                compose—but I'll miss walking home with Emma,
                    and I'm restless: What will I do with myself
                once the applesauce and peas and beans
            are all in their jars on the pantry shelves and
        the storm windows are washed and fitted
back in place, and . . . ? Once I start thinking
        about it, I can see the list goes on and on—help Papa
            butcher the pig and hang the ham and bacon
                in the smokehouse; get all our winter woolens
                    out of storage and check them thoroughly
                for moth holes that need mending; let down
            the hems of all the skirts and dresses
        Grace has outgrown since last winter;
make Christmas gifts for everyone. And then,
        when the earth warms up next April—start all over.
            My life could go on like that forever.
                Unless . . .
                    I hear they need nurses in the army hospitals,
                they need workers in the factories; they're finding
            out that women can do almost all the things
        that men have always done. What if,

some morning, I walk down our path and shut
the gate behind me, keep on going down
the dusty road to town, get on a train to . . .
somewhere? Wouldn't something interesting
be bound to happen?

The Tide That's Drowning Millions
Emma

School isn't much fun
this year without Muriel, without
Ollie. Almost all the boys are gone now.
It's spreading like an epidemic, all of them
following each other into the army, navy, air corps
(they all want to fly), or merchant marines. Whenever
one of the boys signs up, all the rest start talking big;
the teachers applaud the ones who go. Yesterday, Sig
Olsen left (when his sister brags about it, she never
says she tried to talk him out of going, of course).
Frank wrote to us: *They're hoping we can stem
the tide that's drowning millions.* But how,
I begin to wonder, will they set about
doing what no one else has done?

Unbreakable
Muriel

The paper has an article about Aunt Vera's protest.
> The day after she and seven others were arrested,
>> ten new women took their places on the picket line;
>>> those ten were arrested that same day, and fifteen
>>>> more came to hold the banners. The articles
>>> and cartoons are not complimentary—everyone
>> seems to think this is a big joke. When someone takes it
> seriously, it's only to chastise the protesters:

unwomanly, unpatriotic, a thorn in the side of the president
> when he has more important things (The War)
>> to think about. But Aunt Vera managed
>>> to smuggle a letter out of prison. (One of the
>>>> prison workers is secretly on their side.)
>>> *As long as there's a shred of a banner*
>> *to hold up,* Aunt Vera writes, *there will be women*
> *to stand in the rain (or snow, if it comes to that)*

and hold it. We're political prisoners—
> *they are doing their best to break our spirit.*
>> Papa reads it out loud and says, *Good luck to them.*
>>> *My sister's spirit has always been unbreakable.*
>>>> He studies me. *You're a lot like her, Muriel.*
>>> I'm not so sure. Papa thinks I'm strong because
>> I speak up for my beliefs—but as the war
> gets louder all around us, I'm becoming quieter.

If I were in Washington right now, even though
    I'm certain that Aunt Vera and her friends
        are in the right, I'm pretty sure I'd drop the banner
            in the street and slink away before
                I'd let them haul me off to prison.

Names
Ollie

Dig deeper, men, they tell us.
We've been digging five feet deep
through mud, with blisters on our hands, and
still it's raining and the officers command us: *Keep
on digging.* So we do. The walls of this hellhole are all that
stand between us and the gunfire of the enemy. I'm digging furiously,
trying to keep up with Victor, Pete, and Phil. Trying not to think about the
dying men we carried on a makeshift stretcher to the ambulance last night,
and whether they made it to the Red Cross tent. What were their names?
Ron and James, I think, and Douglas. Less than a week ago I said to
Phil, *Tell me your girlfriend's name, and I'll remember it. If
you . . . you know . . . I'll write her a letter.* He said,
*Maeve McGill, in Omaha. What about you,
kid?* Emma, I thought. *No one,* I said.

Against the Dark Space
Muriel

Look, Muriel, five peas in this pod—taste them.
    Saturday afternoon, Grace and I are in the garden
        picking the late summer peas. The sun is warm but not
            too hot, the peas are bursting from their pods,
                and Grace is being good, helping with the work
            without complaining. We need her to be more
        grown-up than usual, more than she probably feels;
she sets her doll, Eliza Jane, at the end of each row
and as she works, she looks up constantly to show me
    and Eliza Jane how many peas she's picked
        (besides the ones she's eating). And so it
            happens that it's Grace who sees him first—
                the man in uniform, turning in our lane.
        I see everything at once—Grace's curiosity,
    until she sees my face shift from calm
to terror, and instantly her face reflects my own.
The man's slow walk, slower still as he approaches.
    The paper in his hand. White against his clean
        blue uniform. (Against the dark space
            of the letters Ollie has not written. Why?)
                Yesterday, I received a short letter from Frank,
        and I see that, too, like a flash of lightning
    across this suddenly dark place.
Grace, I say, *go inside and stay there.*

Tell Mama to come out. Tell her . . .

  No, don't tell her . . . Just say I need her

   in the garden. Somehow I find my way

    to my feet. A fly lands on my wrist, I flick

     it off, it buzzes round my hair, follows

    my slow steps to the gate. Its buzzing drones

   a background to my prayer: *Please, God, please don't*

  let it be true. Don't let it be Ollie. Anything

but that. God. I beg you. Don't

  let it be true. As I reach the gate, Mama

   steps up behind me and speaks one word

    with such authority I feel she could hold back

     a breaking dam with that one word's sheer force.

   No.

  The two of us stand side by side, facing

 the young man, who looks from me to Mama,

back to me, down at his feet. He draws

 in a deep breath before he asks, *Is this the home*

  of Private Frank L. Norman, Jr.?

I Didn't Mean
Muriel

Please forgive me, madam. You say Private Norman lives
    in the next house down the road? I mean . . . He turns red, stammers.
        That is . . . where I will find his family? This man stands before us
            in his uniform, this is his job, he's simply asking
                for directions in an unfamiliar neighborhood—
        but must it be our task to give them? No!
      I want no part of this! Don't tell him, Mama! (Did I
say "anyone but Ollie"? No—I didn't even think that.
Oh, God, you know I didn't mean . . . don't let this be true.
    Please. Send this man back where he came from.)
      Now Mama's quiet voice: *Left at the end*
           of the lane, across the bridge, around a curve
                in the road, you'll see a white house, green shutters.
        Her voice quivers: *Sir? Is it . . . as bad as it seems?*
    He shakes his head and turns away, but we can't tell
  if he's shaking his head no to Mama's question
or only (too gently) refusing to answer it.
    I can get to the Normans' house faster than he can
      by running along the path, crossing the creek
        on the crossing stones. I turn to go, but Mama
          catches my elbow, pulls me close,
        strokes my hair, and whispers,
      Muriel, please stay here
    with Grace.
I'll go.

A Basket
Muriel

Why were you and Mama both so scared
    of that nice man? Grace wants to know.
        I can't think of any way to answer
            but the brutal truth. I kneel beside her,
                push a strand of hair out of her eyes:
                If a soldier is (oh, I want to say "hurt," but Grace
        stares me down) *killed in the war* (she doesn't flinch),
they send someone to your house to tell you.
When he stopped here, we thought he was bringing
    bad news about Ollie. I'm hoping I can stop
        at that, but Grace is quick: *Frank*—she points
            across the creek. *Muriel, does this mean . . . ?*
                I close my eyes and try to think, trying
            at the same time not to think. *I don't know, Grace.*
        Mama has been gone a long time, hasn't she?
        Shall we take our peas to the Normans?
She nods. I gather a few eggs, five peaches,
    all the peas we've picked, and put them in a basket;
        Grace adds a small bouquet of hollyhocks.
            It doesn't help—the more we put into
                the basket, the emptier it seems.

My Shepherd, I Shall Want
Muriel

The Lord is my shepherd, I shall not want.
    Emma repeats over and over, rocking
        back and forth in a corner of their kitchen,
            inconsolable. My arm around her shoulder, I
                absorb the words she speaks, try to separate
            them from her sobs: *I shall not want,*
      I shall not want, the Lord is my shepherd,
    I shall not want. The words twist and turn—
meaning, at the same time, *God willing, I will always have*
    enough of everything I truly need, and *God forbid*
      I should want anything I cannot have. Eventually
          her crying quiets and her voice is still; silence gathers
             like a storm around us—maybe Emma shall not want,
        but I shall. I want Frank to walk through this door.
      I want the door to slam behind him. I want him to be
laughing, making all of us laugh, too. I want to know
where Ollie is; I want both Frank and Ollie home, strong
and whole, sitting right here at this table; and when
      it's time for us to cross the creek and go back home,
         I want Frank and Emma to walk halfway with me and Ollie.
          I want the sun to shine tomorrow morning on Frank's
        brown wavy hair and dimpled smile, and while I'm at it,
    I shall want what I don't even want. I don't expect
to fall in love and I don't plan to marry,

but maybe I want someone
to try to change my mind. Maybe
I've been wondering if that someone
might be Frank. Oh, Emma, Mama,
Mrs. Norman—who will I
not love and marry now?

Nest Blown from Its Tree
Emma

The church is too small to hold so many crying
people. (We save a place where Frank always stood.)
Where did everyone come from, and how did they all hear
about this funeral? My place has been between Frank and Father.
All my life, their voices made a strong, clear arc my voice could climb
up to the rafters, soaring there on its own music, coming home to rest.
Now when the congregation sings this hymn Frank loved—"A Mighty
Fortress Is Our God"—my not-so-mighty voice struggles to take flight
and can't. It gives up, like a bird trying to fly home to a familiar nest
that's been blown from its tree in a storm. Such sudden change: I'm
an only child now, I suppose, one of those odd creatures Mother
feels so sorry for. How will she ever survive? I can hardly bear
to look at her, contorted with the effort to believe in God
on such a day. No doubt asking herself, *Why sing?*

Two Languages
Muriel

A mighty fortress is our God. Those words
      Frank loved so well were written by Martin Luther,
          a German. We sang them at the funeral,
             though it was probably a German soldier who
                killed Frank—can anyone make sense of this?
             Who does God belong to, whose mighty fortress
      is he, if people sing that hymn in two languages,
    and in those same languages defend this war?
Who is the mighty fortress walling in, and who
      does it keep out? A hard rain beats against our window
          for the third day in a row—making mud out of our garden,
             relentless in the way it pounds such questions
                home. And where is Ollie now? Why haven't we
          heard from him these past seven weeks?
          Muriel, you think too much, Mama says. (Am I
    to stop thinking altogether? Would that be more ladylike?)
I have to get out of this house—I go out in the rain,
      walk down the road, and meet the mailman. *Hello, Muriel,*
         he says. *I have a letter for you—from France.* I don't
             even look to see if it's addressed to me. I tear
                it open in the middle of the road, letting the blue
         ink smear in the rain: *Dear Pa and Ma*
    and Muriel and Grace, Thank you for the socks
and cookies. This war is bigger than I expected.

I thought I might see Frank over here, but

    I don't know where he is. Do you?

        It would be awfully nice to see a familiar face.

            Tell Emma I said thank you for her letter.

            I don't have much time to write.

        Your son and brother, Ollie.

      I sob with the relief of hearing from him.

    I know we have to answer. But I won't be

the one to tell him. Let Mama and Papa

    try to find the words—I'd feel like

      I was shooting Ollie in the heart

        if I wrote this awful truth to him:

            You can stop looking.

        Frank was killed in action

      before you even got there.

Staring at Me
Ollie

night again fed myself today

better than last week   ouch

Nurse—   please tie my shoe

(Frank? Where is he?   What happened?)

rat in the trench ran across my arm who killed the rat?

black eyes skinny tail   staring at me

wouldn't stop   explosions   all night

couldn't sleep   losing

track of time how many days weeks?

That's right—you're getting better. At least not any

(tank stuck in mud ambulance)

worse.   *Shall we write a*

letter for you?   *Don't be*

frightened. You'll go home soon.

Invisible Thicket
Muriel

Our home is your home—the Normans' house
    and ours have always felt like two rooms
        in one grand mansion. Now an invisible
            thicket of grief surrounds their house—
                I can barely make myself walk through it.
            In the kitchen, the barn, the fields, Frank's absence
        hovers over everything—he isn't climbing up the windmill
to see who might be coming down the road; he isn't
teasing his mother, pretending to cut into the cake
    she's made for the church supper; he isn't brushing
        burs out of the horses' manes and tails; he isn't
            spreading hot raspberry jam on the first slice
                of bread, warm from the oven; he isn't singing;
            he isn't smiling; he isn't whistling while he mends
        the broken fence where the rooster escaped last night;
    he won't be hitching up his team to drive us all
to the dance next Friday night (he won't ask me to dance—
    the smell of shaving soap, the thoughts we hid so well
        from one another, forever hidden now). The place
            we've tried to hold for Frank to fit back in
                when he returns refuses to close over
            or fill in. It gapes and glares around us everywhere:
        Here I'm not, says Frank, *and here, and here.*

Gray
Emma

It's almost October. Shouldn't
the maple leaves be changing color?
Those four sunflowers must be yellow,
but all the flowers' faces look dirty gray
to me. The purple asters are so brave, trying
to offer us a bit of color while they can, before
they're killed off by the frost. The red rooster's
cock-a-doodle-doo barely wakes me up. It used to
have me jumping out of bed, onto the cool floor,
and getting quickly dressed so I could go flying
downstairs to breakfast. At five a.m. today,
awake already, I clutch my damp pillow,
debating: Should I go to school or
not? Can I still be a student?

A Rock So Heavy
Muriel

Oh, Danny Boy, the pipes, the pipes are calling . . .
Emma is singing, in the middle of the night,
a song we used to sing with Frank and Ollie.
I get up, put on a sweater, and follow
the sweet, sad song through the darkness
to where she is sitting on a tree stump on their side
of the creek, her voice as clear as the rippling water.
I sit down beside her. *I couldn't sleep,* she tells me.
I never can, these days. (I know. I was not asleep myself.)
Nothing, she says, *will ever be the same again.*
I want to comfort her, but everything I think to say
sounds hollow: *The war cannot go on forever?*
(Yes, it can—for Emma, for her parents,
and in a different way for me, it will not end.)
We should be thankful we knew Frank?
(No amount of gratitude can make this loss less heavy.)
Emma, I finally say, *thank you for walking to school*
with Grace this year. She is so proud to be seen
with you—every morning she looks out the window,
waiting for you. When she catches her first glimpse
of you, she starts jumping up and down.
Emma smiles a little—Grace is a ray of light
in all our lives. *It's strange to go to school*
without you, Muriel—nobody stands up

to Mr. Sander the way you did. And so many of the boys
have enlisted over the summer—it's lonely now.
The creek is rushing past. We step to the edge
of the water and Emma tosses in a stone.
Then another, another, and another, each
larger than the one before, until she tries to lift
a rock so heavy she can't budge it, and then she's
crying, and all I can do is help her lift the rock,
swing it back and forth, back and forth again,
until together we can let it go, heaving it
out into the middle of the creek.

Blinding Light
Ollie

Just to check—a nightmare?
Stump of an arm? Does the pain mean
this all might be real? Pa's letter . . . here it is.
"Frank was killed in action, Friday, August 31."
That can't be true. Frank—my closest friend! No.
I will wake up soon. *Nurse, what am I doing here?*
Shot just below my shoulder? Recuperating well?
Not possible. I'd remember that. *Yes, it's true—*
while trying to save a wounded man. It was a
rat, not a man, I helped into a trench. *No, a*
tank was coming. Philip Ross—you saved
his life. Someone had a rifle. I tried to
jump into the trench. An explosion
burst. *You're lucky to be alive.*

A Bullet and a Bandage
Muriel

Emma, I say, *you look like you've seen a ghost.*
    What is it? She opens her mouth to speak,
        but can't, reaching out instead to give me
            a sealed letter, addressed to me—in Frank's
                handwriting. It's my turn to be speechless.
            The Army sent a box of Frank's personal effects,
    Emma tells me, trembling. *I found this tucked*
into his Bible. My parents haven't seen it—
I won't mention it to them unless you ask me to.
    She gives my hand a squeeze, then leaves me alone.
        I open the envelope, take out the letter
            (several sheets of paper). *August 27, 1917.*
                Dear Muriel, Frank began, as if it were one
            of a hundred letters he would write to me.
    They'll censor much of what I want to say,
but it might do me some good to say it anyway.
Save my letters, and when I come home I'll fill in
the missing lines for you. The rest of the letter
        may as well have passed through the censors' hands—
            I can't read it through my tears. When I can stop
                crying, I read on: *I was well trained,* he wrote.
        I thought I understood why we were over here,
    what we are being asked to do. At first, it made
some kind of sense. I even thought I'd be able

to explain it to you, and maybe change your mind
  about our being here. But more often than not these days,
    you are the one who changes my mind. Your words
      come back to me when I have to pull a trigger, or
        when I can't sleep after killing someone. "Why
      is everyone just doing what they're told?"
    you asked, that night after your graduation. Sometimes
I find that hard to answer. I blink, back up, read again:
"after killing someone." Frank killed someone.

More than once? I take a deep breath, read on:
      We're lined up on one side of a line, other soldiers
        line up facing us, and then we shoot each other.
          That's about the size of it. When you read
        about the war in the papers over there, it sounds
      like we spend our days moving lines around a map,
half an inch a week. It's easier to make sense
of who's the enemy and who is on our side.
But when you see a soldier lying facedown
  in the mud and he's been there a few days
    and everyone is marching past him because
      no one has the time to move him, or give him
    a proper burial—maybe say a simple prayer
  over his body—it barely matters what kind of
uniform he's wearing. Dead bodies
look and smell the same, whatever side
  they once were on. I know I shouldn't question
    what I'm doing; they drill it into us: "A split
      second can mean the difference between
        killing the enemy and being killed."
      But do I want to lose that part of myself

that insists on taking stock of what I'm doing
every time I do it? That's hard to answer, Muriel.
I'll put this letter away for a few days,
and then decide if I should mail it.
If you're reading it at all, no matter what
they've crossed out before it comes to you,
at least you'll know that I was thinking of you.
Your friendship gives me comfort
through long nights in the trenches.
I hope this finds you well, my dear.
With love, Frank.

A bullet and a bandage for the wound
it causes, all in one small envelope.
My questions may have caused a hesitation
that cost Frank his . . . his certainty.
His life? However long I live, it won't
be long enough to silence that suggestion.
I stuff the letter deep into my pocket
("my dear" . . . "with love")
and walk to Reuben Lake. A harsh wind
whips up the water's surface; somewhere
among the whitecaps' tumult, a loon
cries out. Hard as I listen for an answer,
there is none.

86

Applesauce
Muriel

Bushels of red apples,
        knife against my thumb,
                peelings curling in a pile
                        on the floor. Grace's chatter.
                                Mama's admonitions and advice.
                        You're awfully quiet, Muriel.
                        What's wrong with you today?
        Emma and her mother
stir the apples, keep
        the pot from boiling over.
                (Thank you, Emma,
                        for the question you
                                refrain from asking.)
                        I have burned
                the letter. I will never
        tell a soul what it contained.

White Shirt Crumpled in the Mud

October 1917

Her Careful Signature
Muriel

Another letter from Aunt Vera—disappointing,
    and peculiar. *My dear ones,* it begins,
        As you may know, We are still here: you
            Have probably finished your canning by now.
                Has the pastor Stopped by to see you lately?
            I hope to be Eating Thanksgiving dinner with you
    next month. And then her careful signature.
Papa puzzles over it—why doesn't she tell us
what is happening in prison? She must know we're worried.
Mama pulls her lips into a tight line.
    Papa hands me the letter, and I read it four times.
        It's not like Aunt Vera, I point out, *to make errors*
            in capitalization. That's her job, as a secretary,
        to correct the errors other people make.
    We analyze the words she has mis-capitalized:
We . . . Have . . . Stopped . . . Eating. A hunger strike?
It's the only power they have—to refuse
    what their jailers try to feed them.
        Papa runs his hands through his hair, leans against
            the door, and lets out a long, low whistle.
            These women mean what they say, he says.
        This could go on awhile. It could get worse.
    What is Papa saying? They can't refuse
to eat forever—can they? If they could,

no one would let them die of starvation—would they?
    Either the president will issue an order
            to release them, or the women will start eating.
                    I can't imagine (though I can't stop trying)
                    how it could get worse.

I Know Instantly
Muriel

Ollie! I'm hanging out the clothes,
    pinning Papa's church shirt to the line,
        and I look up to see the merest speck
            off in the distance, coming closer. I know
                instantly it's Ollie—I recognize him by
            the rhythm of his walk. I drop the white shirt
        in the mud and run so hard I'm barely breathing
    by the time I'm close enough to see his smile.
I throw my arms around his neck and he
    sets down his duffel bag and puts . . .
        one arm . . . around me . . .
            Across my left shoulder and around my back,
                the absence of Ollie's right arm spreads
            icy fingers over me. I pull away and stare—
        not at my brother's face (all I saw
    when I ran to him)—no, not at Ollie's face,
but at the sleeve pinned to his shirt. I blurt
    out my question, *Where's your arm?* and he
        draws in a breath, as if to answer quickly
            before the question finds a way to push
                the two of us apart. But then there's Mama.
        She's been running, too, her hands white
    with flour, and before Ollie has a chance to answer,
Mama sweeps my words away: *Muriel,* she gasps,

what kind of question is that?
    It's the same kind of question as the look
        on her face—joy and horror, pride and
            anger, all rolled into one. She looks at Ollie's
                empty sleeve, and at his face. She doesn't give
        the smallest glance in my direction
      even as she shushes me. *Oliver,* she says,
    we praise the good Lord you've returned.
She puts her arm through the elbow he still has,
    and turns with him toward home.
        I hope Ollie doesn't notice, when I reach
            for his other hand, how my hand flutters
                back down to my side like a sparrow
            shot out of the sky. I pick up Ollie's duffel bag
        and walk along beside him. Mama chatters
    all the way home—so that I won't, I suppose.
Or—so that Ollie doesn't have to?

Blackberry Jam
Emma

Stirring jam in a cast-iron pot,
I see, through the window, Muriel run
up the hill. She slows to a walk, then, barely
moving, approaches our door. I have never known
Muriel to hesitate when she comes into our house. I
open the door. *Is something wrong?* (Though there is
also a deep joy in her eyes.) *Muriel . . . what is it? Has
something happened?* She starts to answer me just as,
behind us on the stove, the sugar and blackberries
boil over. Mother comes rushing in: *Emma, why
did you stop stirring?* Then she has her own
reaction to Muriel's expression. She stares
as Muriel answers: *Ollie is home. One
arm is . . .* She can't finish. *What?*

Mud
Muriel

Late afternoon, bitter wind,
    eight pairs of socks half frozen
        on the line, Papa's white shirt
            crumpled in the mud where I
                dropped it when I ran to Ollie—
            yes, I have to wash it out again.
        I have to rinse it, wring it out,
    and hang it on the line to dry.
I am not complaining—
    look what I can do—I hold the shirt
        with one hand while I reach
            for a clothespin with the other!
            Oh, Ollie . . .

Changes
Ollie

Raspberries have come and gone.
Rows of cornstalks stand like soldiers:
one strong wind could blow them all down.
I was in the war for three weeks, not counting
the time in the hospital, and everything is different
now. Muriel and Grace ask if I want to join them in a
card game. *Sure,* I say, *I'll shuffle. Oh . . . um, let's play
partners. Here, Muriel—you can shuffle.* I keep looking
down at my sleeve and thinking of things I won't ever
be able to do again: tie a fishing fly, hammer in a nail.
Why me? I ask Pa. He looks at me long and hard.
*Son, that question leads nowhere. These old
crows around here still know you. The
past is past. You're home now.*

This Changes Everything
Muriel

At least you have your brother home,
  Emma says, which means I can't talk
    to her about my horror. I keep picturing
      the moment Ollie's arm was torn from him . . .
        What did it look like? How close did he
      come to dying? He says he can't remember,
    but maybe he remembers in some awful,
  wordless way. He's sleeping all the time—
Mama says he's healing, and we should
  let him be. Beyond that, she doesn't say
    a word about the way this changes
      everything for all of us. What does Mama do
        with rage she thinks she shouldn't feel?
      If God knows what he's doing, and
    the president is worthy of our trust,
  where does Mama look for reasons
to explain why she is cutting Ollie's food
  the way she used to do when he
    was two years old?

Take This Bread
Emma

Everything that used to be easy is hard.
We've always run so freely across the creek and back.
Now when I say, *Let's go over to welcome Ollie home,* Mother
answers, *I'm sorry, Emma, I can't, just yet. You go. Take this bread.*
I would give my own right arm, she says, *to have Fra— I'll go when . . .*
Well, I don't know when, exactly. Mother simply can't, so I go alone, and
find: Ollie asleep, Muriel scolding her hens as she throws them their grain,
Grace clutching her doll in her playhouse, and Mrs. Jorgensen cleaning a rain
gutter, scrubbing at it with such ferocity she slices the palm of her left hand
on the sharp edge, shakes off the blood, but doesn't stop to wash it. Then
she goes right back to work, oblivious. I offer the bread: *Mother said*
to give you this. She'd have come, but she had to . . . do some other
things. Mrs. Jorgensen stares at me. *Shouldn't you wash that*
cut? I ask. *Oh . . . yes.* Her blood drips across the yard.

Phantom Pain
Ollie

Pain in a missing limb is common,
Pa tells me. *They call it phantom pain.* An itch I
can't scratch. I try to imagine some way a mosquito could
bite an arm that isn't there, but it's so obviously not possible.
None of this makes sense. And another thing—or the same thing?
Why does the sight of our pigs wallowing in mud behind the barn
send me running into the house for shelter like we're coming to the
end of the world? I've never been afraid of pigs! I see them in their
sty after a rain, and I start to shudder so hard I can barely stand up.
One image—pigs in mud—immediately brings another: dark
night, heavy rain, a muddy boot. And then my mind goes
blank. Pa says, *It's hard not to think about such things.*
Ma says, *Leave the war behind now. Rest your*
brain. But my brain won't rest.

What Kind of Luck?
Muriel

Everyone is telling Ollie not to think
    the things he can't help thinking.
        Mama cautions me: *Don't mention anything*
            that will remind him of the war. But what if
                Ollie *wants* to tell someone what happened,
        like Frank tried to tell me those hard
    things he couldn't say to anyone in France
or in letters to his family? *Let's go out*
for a walk, I suggest to Ollie, after supper.
    We walk in near silence for an hour—a few
        small comments about the calves, the land,
            the weather. When we come to the pigsty
                Ollie sharply looks away, walks faster.
        As we approach the gate, I stop myself
    from reaching out to open it for him, and he finds
a way to unlatch it, swing it open, catch it, and close it
behind us with one hand. We keep walking, our footsteps
    falling in a steady rhythm. Eventually
        Ollie breaks our silence with one word:
            Lucky, he mutters. And then, *I'm supposed*
                to feel lucky because I still have one arm.
        (Luckier than Frank—I regret the thought
    the second it crosses my mind.) *What kind of luck*
is that, Ollie asks, *to go through life*

thinking about all the ways it could be worse?
I could have lost both arms, both legs, I could
be blind and deaf, I could have burns on my face
so bad you wouldn't know me, I could be nuts,
I could be
dead.
I saw all those things, he tells me,
in the army hospital. Are they supposed to cheer me up?
Muriel, I'm telling you—he searches for words—
this stinks. I try my best to think of something
wise and comforting to say.
Yes, Ollie, is all I can come up with,
it sure does.

A Few Sentences Each Day
Muriel

Every afternoon (five days in a row now),
    Ollie and I take a walk together—today
        we follow Crabapple Creek all the way
           to Reuben Lake, the rhythm of our steps
              accompanied by small sounds of birds,
          chipmunks, a family of raccoons, the crunch
      of dry leaves, and, when we reach the lake,
the back-and-forth lament of a pair of loons.
Returning home along the road, Ollie
    glances toward the school. *What time*
        is it? he asks. *One o'clock,* I answer. *Grace and Emma*
           won't be out for two more hours. Ollie turns his face
           away from me; he may be embarrassed
        that I've guessed he's thinking about Emma.
      I don't know if I'll ever graduate, he says.
    I can't seem to think straight; my mind keeps
wandering back to things I don't know how
    to think about. A horse whinnies and comes over
        to the fence; Ollie pulls up a handful of grass
           and feeds him. *Animals always seem to trust you,*
          I say. He nods and starts to speak, but
      doesn't. A shudder passes over him, and
    we walk home in silence—not the kind where
two people are so comfortable that nothing

needs to be spoken, the kind where
      something is trying to be said
          and no one knows the words.
               As soon as we get home, Ollie
                    goes into his room, shuts the door,
              and stays there until dinner.

Daisies on a Pillowcase
Emma

Mother needs a good, reliable friend
these days, more than she ever has. I wish she would
go with me to the Jorgensens'. Each day she says, *I'll go tomorrow.*
She's been embroidering daisies on a pillowcase for five weeks! *It's best
not to push her,* Mrs. Jorgensen says. *Your mother can't talk about Frank yet,
but she probably can't think about anything else. Be patient, Emma, grief takes time.*
Yes, but so does my schoolwork plus cooking and washing dishes and hanging clothes
and dusting furniture and cleaning out the horses' stalls. While Mother grieves, those
endless tasks aren't doing themselves. Has Father, or anyone, even noticed that I'm
doing most of Mother's work, all my own, and half of Frank's? Will *I* ever get
time to grieve for my brother? (And, in a way, for Ollie.) When can *I* rest?
Now I'm ashamed of this anger—a mix of exhaustion and sorrow
that bubbles up, then settles down. Here comes Ollie. Could
he help stack the firewood? I have clothes to mend.

The Phone Rings: Two Short, One Long
Muriel

I'm home alone, except for Ollie,
    who is sleeping at noon on a Monday
        while Mama and Papa are at work.
            The phone rings: two short, one long—
                our ring on the party line. *You have*
            a long-distance call, the operator says,
        from Washington, D.C. (Could it be Aunt Vera?)
    Hello, am I speaking to Mrs. Jorgensen? (Danish accent,
a younger woman, not Aunt Vera's voice.)
    No, I answer, *this is Muriel, her daughter.*
        May I help you? A slight pause, then,
            I am wanting to speak to Mr. Jorgensen,
                Vera's brother. I tell her I'm home alone.
            Can you give to your father a message for me?
    (No, I'm tempted to reply, we've had all
the bad news we can take.) *Of course,* I answer,
picking up a pencil. *My name,* she says,
    is Ruby Madsen. I am living
        in Washington, and I have been
            picketing the White House with Vera.
                She is in prison for five weeks now.
    (Five weeks? I've lost track of time!)
    They are beginning to see they can't
prison us forever—they release a few

women already. Vera still refuse to eat,
no matter how hard things are for her.
You know how strong she is in her mind,
but in her body she is very weak now.
We are hoping they release her next week,
but she can't travel alone then. I want to ask
your father can he come to Washington
to travel home with his sister. Ruby gives me
a number where she can be reached, and asks me
to have Papa call her back or send a telegram.
I'll give him the message, I promise.
I stay on the line to find out how many
people have been listening in.
Two clicks—no, three. Who else, besides
the operator, heard our conversation?
I hitch up the horses as quickly as I can—
I want to reach the lumberyard and give Papa
this message before he hears it as the gossip
it will become within the hour.

Muriel Can Help
Muriel

I don't see how I can go, Papa says to Mama.
　　We're shorthanded at work as it is these days.
　　　　He studies Mama's face. *Could you go?* he asks.
　　　　　　Mama shakes her head. *It's all too much; I'm
　　　　　　　　going to quit my job—Ollie needs me at home.
　　　　　　But that's the reason I can't do this for Vera.
　　　　　　How could I be away for a week right now?
　　Ollie objects—he's finally woken up, after sleeping
for twelve hours a day, six days in a row—*I have to*
　　learn to take care of myself sometime, Ma.
　　　　　　Go ahead, if you want to—Muriel can help me.
　　　　　　Mama glances from me to Ollie, and then
　　　　　　　　　to Papa; she opens her mouth, closes it—
　　　　　　she doesn't want to go, she's hurt that Ollie
　　　　doesn't think he needs her, and neither she,
　　nor anyone, questions Ollie's assumption
that "Muriel can help." They all know
　　　　　　I'll do what's asked of me, in this, as always. I see
　　　　　　　　in that glance a long lifetime ahead of me—am I to be
　　　　　　　　　　"my brother's keeper"? His right arm? Even as
　　　　　　I'm forming words, about to spill them out,
　　　　I'm wary of hurting Ollie and Mama,
　　wishing Papa would come to my defense

before I say things I'll regret—and then Grace,
     sitting quietly, combing out the tangles in
        Eliza Jane's long hair, looks around
           at all of us. *Maybe Mama could stay home,*
          she says, *and Muriel could go.*

Crazy Ideas
Muriel

Sometimes the most obvious idea remains
     hidden, and when it shows itself like this,
        we all wonder how we missed it.
              Within a day, it's settled: I'll take the train
                to Washington, D.C., next Tuesday, meet
            Aunt Vera and travel home with her.
      She'll come here and rest for a few days,
    then continue on her own, back to Chicago.
Papa jokes about Aunt Vera's friends: *Radicals,*
    freethinkers—be careful not to come home with too
        many crazy ideas, Muriel. He's smiling, but does he
              mean it, too? I'd bet anything he had to convince Mama,
                and now he's warning me about her worries.
            Emma has come for supper (without her parents—
        Not quite yet, she said to Mama). Sitting between
    Grace and Ollie, she heartily approves.
Go ahead, Muriel—I can help with your chores
    while you're away. And Grace chimes in,
        I will, too, Muriel. Go to Washington! Come home
            with all the crazy ideas you want. A shadow
              passes over Ollie's face, but he says nothing
            at the time—it's only later, after we've walked
      home with Emma, and the two of us are coming back
    together, that I realize how worried Ollie is,

how much he counts on me since he's been home.
I'll only be gone a week, I try to reassure him.
I know, he says. *It's just that you're the only one
who lets me talk about what happened
over there.* He pauses at the gate,
leans his weight against it, glances
up at me—yes, he sees, I'm listening.
I'm starting to remember things, he tells me.

Ollie's Patchwork Story
Muriel

A rat with a man's face, Ollie says. *Or a man*
        with the face of a rat. I don't know which.
                I hated those filthy rats. They scurried
                        through the trenches, tried to chew into
                                our rations, got into our bedrolls.
                        Then one night, I was eating, and I looked
                up to see one staring at me. I saw its hunger,
        and I was hungry, too, and then in that same
moment, a man behind me threw a stone
        and hit it, and it leaped into the air and
                tried to run and couldn't, and it curled up
                        and died. Ollie is struggling not to cry;
                                he's determined to say what he can see
                        while he can see it. *There was a tank*
                rolling toward us—was it that same day?
        It's all packed together in my mind, it's hard
to separate. The nurse in the army hospital
        told me I carried my buddy Phil out
                of harm's way; I saved his life, she said,
                        before I lost my arm. I don't remember that.
                                I remember a soldier coming toward me
                        with his rifle pointed at my chest. He looked
                at me—he saw me, Muriel. The rat was hungry,
        he was hungry. Did that soldier see that I was

hungry, too? Of course he could have killed me.
But he didn't—I had my rifle strapped
across my shoulder. He must have had
a moment of compassion—I don't remember
this—but think about it, Muriel. A
German soldier looked me in the eye
and didn't kill me. Instead—I've thought
long and hard about that moment—my
enemy decided to . . . disarm me.

A Sharp Yes-and-No Shoots Through Me

November 1917

Toward—I Don't Know What
Muriel

Mama's birthday is coming up, Grace says. *Take this,*
   and add it to your egg money—see if it's enough
      to buy her a new hat in Washington. She gives me
         all her money, a stream of warm coins poured
            from one of her old socks into my hands.
      All of it? I ask. *Yes!* She's certain. Grace
   almost makes me want to stay right here
with her and Ollie and Mama and Papa—
I start to think of everything I'll miss. But my suitcase
   is packed, and Papa calls out, *We don't have*
      all day. I hug Grace—*Thank you. I'll be home*
         in eight days. Help Mama all you can.
            I ride to town with Papa, buy my ticket,
         board the train, and wave goodbye.
   And then the whistle blows and I'm carried
out of the life I know, toward—I don't know what.
The world goes by outside—we pass farms like ours:
   a girl no taller than Grace leads three cows to pasture;
      a young man rides his horse along a rough dirt road;
         a woman holds two chickens she's just killed,
            her large hands encircling their necks;
      a little boy waves at us and grins when I wave back.
   At every stop, young men get on the train,
their mothers weeping as they say goodbye: soldiers,

sailors, whole and bright-eyed like Frank and Ollie were

five months ago. I want to jump out of my seat

and stop them: *Stay where you are, stay home!*

Don't go to war! Everyone around me

is offering them food, thanking them

for things they haven't even done yet.

The young men soak up the admiration,

stand a little taller. It isn't that they're foolish—

I'm sure they're brave and smart.

But they don't know what's coming.

They haven't seen the look in Ollie's eyes

as he struggles to recall what happened;

they haven't tried to comfort Mrs. Norman.

Here with Grace
Ollie

Who's to say I can't? I have an arm, a left foot, a
right foot. We set up a system: rope, hook, and pulley.
Pa encourages me: *I don't see why it shouldn't work.* He's sure I
can lift a bale of hay from down here on the barn floor up into the
loft—*I'll be there to pull it up and over,* he says. I'm here with Grace,
who watches from a safe distance—I'm determined to do this by myself. I
lay the rope straight out on the ground and use my arm and feet to roll the
hay bale onto it. Holding the rope in place with one foot, I can tie a knot. I
do that twice, then hook the bale to the pulley rope. (It's not hard, I've
often done this.) I sit on the rope's other end as I reach and pull. *A
man is more than arms and legs,* Pa said. (Tell that to Emma.)
Ma argued: *It's too much to attempt at this point.* (She
might be right.) The bale rises—I'm scared I'll
lose it. I don't. *I've got it!* Pa calls down.

Look Deeper
Muriel

These buildings—they're enormous!
How could people build something so high?
This is Washington, D.C.! I've never seen so many
people in one place—everyone rushing about
as if they have important business.
That lady's hat is three times the size of her head—
it must take a hundred hat pins to hold it in place!
Ruby Madsen meets me at the station; I recognize her
by her gold-and-purple suffrage sash, her long black curls,
just as she described herself. She's not much older than I am.
You must be Muriel! Are you hungry? Yes, and yes—
we go to the station café and sit down.
We are expecting Vera to be release tomorrow,
Ruby tells me. *Until then, I show you around.*
Will you like to see National Woman's Party
headquarters while you're here? I nod—there is so much
to see! Ruby has been in America for two years; she came
on her own from Denmark when she was seventeen.
I'd like to hear her whole life story, but she's
anxious to get back to the picket line.
As we leave the café, I feel a tug at my skirt—
a girl about four years old, with dirty tear streaks
down her face, holds out her hand to me. I reach
into my pocket for a coin, but Ruby shakes her head

as we walk on. *It's a bad idea,* she says,
　　to courage beggar children. This is not
　　　a safe place for them—someone use
　　　　that little girl. The child's face
　　　　　stays with me—shouldn't someone
　　　　　help her? As we move through the station,
　　　　more children approach us, two boys, another
　　little girl, then an old man in tattered clothes
who looks so hungry I give him the apple
I still have from home—*Bless you, miss,* he says.
　　　I smile, but almost immediately a woman
　　　　carrying a baby holds out her hand,
　　　　　and I don't have another apple. People
　　　　　who look like they have plenty of food and money
　　　　walk past and no one begs from them. *Why is everyone*
asking me? I ask Ruby. She studies me: *You have*
a kind face, she answers. Outside the station,
　　we get into an electric streetcar that pulls us along
　　　the tracks, without horses. The streets are so busy—
　　　　hundreds of buggies, motorcars, bicycles,
　　　　　young men and women walking arm in arm.
　　　　I'm dizzy from looking. We pass a row of mansions
　　with grand doorways and white pillars;
then gradually things change—smaller houses,
dirty streets. *Just two more blocks,*
　　Ruby says. It's hard to describe what I see.
　　　　This neighborhood . . . it looks . . . so . . . I pause.
　　　　Poor? Ruby suggests. I nod, a little embarrassed.
　　　　Look deeper, she says. (A rat runs by.
　　　Something smells bad. Mama would call the children

"little ragamuffins.") A woman comes out of a brick
building, surrounded by four small children; they wave
and smile at us—at Ruby, really, but I'm included, too.
This, Ruby tells me, *is the settlement house*
where I live and teach kindergarten.
I've heard about settlement houses: people,
mostly women, live in a neighborhood where
there is work to be done—cleaning up the streets,
taking care of children, building playgrounds,
helping new immigrants get settled in America.
We stop here long enough for you to fresh up,
then, if you like, I take you over to
the White House. (For half a second, I could be
one of ten thousand tourists, and she my
gracious guide.) *I thought you will*
be interested, she goes on, *in meeting*
your Aunt Vera's friends—the women
on the picket line. A sharp yes-and-no
shoots through me. Yes, I want to meet
these women—I want to find out for myself
if they are dangerous, misguided, unpatriotic.
And, no, I'm not prepared to stand with Ruby
and the others in the White House picket line,
where I could be arrested. I'm here to take
Aunt Vera home, not to join her and her friends—
however brave they are—in prison.

Could I?
Muriel

As Ruby and I walk to the White House,
    I ask her how she met Aunt Vera. *I meet her*
        in Chicago, she tells me, *just after I come*
            from Denmark. I have never been in so large a city.
            I sleep the first night in Union Station,
        alone and very frighten. A rough-looking man
      come up to me next morning. "You need
  a place to stay?" he ask. "Come with me."
I know not enough English to understand
  what he is suggesting. I try to ignore him,
      but he follow me—I am close to cry when Vera
        walk right up, just like she know me:
            "Oh, there you are," she say, in English—
        but I can hear Danish in her accent!
    "I'm sorry to be late," she say. "Your father
  was delay and he can't meet you. Come along
home now." That man disappear like a mouse into a
hole in the wall! I never see Vera before in my life,
    but she introduce herself, speaking Danish,
        and then she bring me to Hull House—
            you know it? A settlement house in Chicago.
      They helping me so much, I want to help
  other people, and when I hear they need teacher
in Washington, I come, and now I'm here ten month.

Vera always stay with me when she come to Washington.
She find my name in English because people
can't pronounce my Danish name, Ragnhild.
I smile at that—it *is* hard to pronounce.
I don't think I could do what Ruby has done.
I think about waking up at home: the smell of biscuits
and fried eggs, the rooster's boisterous "good morning,"
the whisper of Crabapple Creek against the stones. *I've lived*
in the same place since I was born, I tell Ruby,
and soon I'm telling her all about my life,
as if it is as interesting as her own. She asks me
questions about Frank and Ollie, Mr. Sander;
I tell her I despise this war, but I hardly ever
dare to say so. *I wish women could vote,*
I venture, and Ruby answers, *Wishing*
won't happen it. We've walked
two and a half miles. *Look—the White House.*
It's even bigger, more imposing than it appears
on picture postcards. It makes the women
standing with their banners at the gate
look awfully small, but when Ruby
introduces me to them, each one in turn
smiles and miraculously becomes a giant.

Picket Line
Muriel

A light snow is falling as I meet
    the women on the picket line—
        Lucinda Schultz wears her hair like Emma's;
            Mrs. Ellis reminds me of my fourth-grade teacher;
                Mary McGill tilts her head to one side, like
            the Normans' photograph of Great-aunt Sarah.
        Some of these women are Mama's age, some are closer
to mine; some wear expensive fur coats, others threadbare cloth.
Ruby steps into the line to hold a banner with Lucinda:
DENMARK ON THE VERGE OF WAR GAVE WOMEN THE VOTE.
    WHY NOT GIVE IT TO AMERICAN WOMEN NOW?
        I don't join the line; I stand aside to watch.
           When four young men approach the picketers,
        a crowd gathers, watching and cheering—clearly they
    expect something to happen. A little girl stands on tiptoe
peering through the crowd, and her mother pulls
her back, glancing at the women in the picket line
    as if they, and not the four young men, are dangerous.
        A short man pushes a tall man toward Ruby,
           taunting, *You're a good-lookin' gal—*
                you need a man? Here's one for you.
        Ruby holds her banner high, ignoring them,
    even when the tall man stumbles and falls
in front of her. The short man doesn't help him up;

he laughs and says, *Elmer here, he falls for every*

pretty girl he sees, then looks around, expecting us to laugh

at this pathetic joke. When no one, including Elmer,

does, he grabs a banner and runs off with it.

Five bucks is five bucks, he hollers back,

as Elmer scrambles to his feet and follows him.

(Someone is paying these men to torment

the picketers? Five dollars for a stolen

banner? Where are the police?)

The crowd grows larger, noisier. I'm relieved

when the police arrive, assuming they'll arrest

the most belligerent of these men—those two,

who have obviously been drinking, or that one,

shaking his fist in Lucinda Schultz's face.

Yes, two officers approach Lucinda, take her

by both arms, and escort her away from the drunken man.

(She does not appear to appreciate their protection.)

You're under arrest, they say (what? to her?)

as the man who has been threatening her

laughs and walks away. Ruby is left alone,

trying to hold the banner by herself—

I pause only for a second before

stepping in and picking up the other side

as Lucinda grips the police wagon's iron bars

and Ruby asks the officer, *What is she charge with?*

He replies, *The same as usual: obstructing traffic.*

But we're not obstructing anything—

we're standing well back on the sidewalk,

and the traffic is obstructed only by the

crowd. Why don't the police control

the crowd? A WOMAN'S PLACE IS IN THE HOME.
A man holds up a wide, flat board with that slogan
scrawled across it in large letters, and something
I can't quite read in small writing below it. *A plank
for your platform,* he taunts. He waves the board
at Ruby and me—we pretend not to notice.
The crowd surges forward, meaner now.
I squint to read the small words on the plank:
BAREFOOT AND PREGNANT IN THE KICHEN
(he can't spell "kitchen"). I think: Papa
and Mr. Norman—with Frank and Ollie's help—
built the barn in twenty days, nailing down
each plank so carefully. (How will Ollie
use a hammer now?) These men are neither
building anything nor fighting overseas.
Much as I despise the war, I despise
them even more. I face the man and
speak. My voice is clear and strong:
You are a lazy coward.
Ruby stares at me, the look
on her face my only warning—
the man raises the plank
above his head
(he's tall, I'm short);
the board cracks
on my head . . .
my knees buckle . . .
loud buzzing . . .
black . . . spinning stars . . .
distant voices . . .

Sash Abandoned in the Snow
Muriel

I open my eyes and look around.
　　The man who hit me has disappeared—
　　　　into the paddy wagon, I assume
　　　　　　(the police are locking it).
　　　　　　　　Ruby and Mrs. Ellis help me to my feet.
　　　　　　Are you needing an ambulance? asks Ruby.
　　　　No, I answer, *I'll be okay in a minute.*
　　The crowd is dispersing, but . . .
all these banners on the ground, and . . .
　　Where are the picketers? I ask.
　　　　Ruby points to the paddy wagon
　　　　　　driving off. Not the brutal man inside,
　　　　　　　　but eleven peaceful women. *Why?* I ask.
　　　　　　"Obstructing traffic," Ruby mimics.
　　　　Mrs. Ellis gathers up the banners.
　　She'll need help carrying them back to
headquarters. A lump is rising on my forehead
　　as I kneel to pick up a gold-and-purple sash—
　　　　torn, abandoned in the snow. I fold it
　　　　　　carefully and put it in my pocket.

Grace Brings a Message
Emma

Grace brings a message on the day
we thought Muriel would be coming home.
Muriel got hurt. She was in a suffering picket line.
Aunt Vera isn't out yet. They won't be home until next week.
She must mean "suffrage." My first thought, unfortunately, is not:
What happened to Muriel? Oh, I'm so sorry! How badly is she hurt?
But rather: Another long week of doing half of her work, plus my own.
Grace looks tired. She's doing as much as she can; I don't want to moan
to her about this—she's a child. I go back to the ironing. Father's shirt
is missing its top button—where is it? Then Grace says, *I'm hot,*
Emma. Will you walk partway with me—as far as the creek?
It's been too long since I, or any of us, have made time
for Grace. Wait a minute—her face . . . How come
it's so red? *Yes, I'll walk you home,* I say.

We're Winning
Muriel

The goose egg on my head has gone down.
    Ruby and I wait with Mrs. Ellis at the prison gate—
        I'm telling them about Aunt Vera: *When she*
            comes to visit, she always brings a book for me, a toy
                for Grace. She brings Ollie chocolates,
            and something practical for Papa—a handsaw
        or a box of nails. For Mama, she finds a new hat
    or dress—the latest fashion from Chicago.
Mama always says, "Oh, I could never
    wear something so flamboyant, Vera—you
        keep it; it looks better on you." But in the end,
            Mama usually keeps her gift;
                occasionally she even wears it.
        I'm smiling at these memories, picturing
      Aunt Vera getting off the train last Christmas
    in her blue wool coat and matching hat,
sweeping me into a big hug . . .
    Here she is. What does Mrs. Ellis mean?
        I see the prison gate swing open—
            but here *who* is? The woman
                who walks toward us on the arm
            of a prison matron is so thin her coat
    is hanging off her shoulders.
Her hair is limp and oily, tied back

with a filthy scarf. Only when she leaves
the matron and comes to take my arm
do I recognize Aunt Vera, flashing
her familiar smile with the words:
We're winning.

An Angel from Heaven
Muriel

Aunt Vera needs a few days to regain
    her strength. *Horrible, just horrible.*
        I'll tell you more about it when I can.
           While I'm here, I'm helping out in Ruby's
                kindergarten class. I love the children!
           At six-thirty Wednesday morning, a mother
        brings her child to the door. *Could you look after*
Joey until school starts this morning? she asks.
No, I'm sorry, Ruby answers. *I need time for making*
    my classroom ready to all the children.
        The mother walks away, pulling Joey along.
           She looks so tired and discouraged, I can't
                imagine how anyone could refuse her.
           If I let him come in, Ruby explains, *they are all*
    arriving an hour early every day. But surely
    it can't do any harm if *I* help, just this once.
I run to catch up with them: *I'll watch him for you.*
    The mother looks like she might cry. *Oh, thank you, miss—*
        you're an angel from heaven. Joey tentatively
           takes my hand. We walk back to the playground.
                Ma has to go to work, he says. *If she's late,*
    they'll give her job to someone else.
    I don't like to go with her—it's cold
where she works! His shoelace is broken; the pieces

are in knots; the shoe is falling off his foot.

    I have an extra shoelace in my suitcase—

        I get it for him and help him loosen the knots

            so we can take the old one out and put the new one in.

              He watches me tie it, then tries it himself,

           and keeps on trying until he can do it.

        Such a simple thing—a shoelace—but by the time

    he's tied his shoe, he's grinning, and all day

in Ruby's class, he won't leave my side.

    When Ruby tells a story, he sits close beside me;

        when the children go outdoors, he takes my hand

            to keep me with him. And when his mother

              comes to pick him up, he unties his shoe,

           ties it, beams up at her. *Miss Muriel*

    teached me how, he says.

Put Grace on My Back
Ollie

Stone by stone, Emma crosses carefully,
so she won't stumble and fall in the water—carrying
Grace in her arms! Why? I run to them. *Ollie, Grace fainted. I
need your help,* she says. *I am so happy to see you!* I wade right in, up
to my knees in the cold water, lean down so Emma can put Grace on
my back, and then I reach back with my arm to hold her there. Emma,
walking close beside me (right through the water, not on the stones),
talks softly, stretches her arm across Grace's back, holding her (and
by chance, holding me). *What's wrong with her? Maybe it's that
flu that's going around,* I whisper. Emma shudders. *Did you
read the article about it in this morning's paper? I can't
face the thought,* she says. (Pa's not home. Could I
go for the doctor?) Ma sees us and rushes out,
Oh, no, she cries. *No! Not our Grace!*

Nothing to Do with Nourishment
Muriel

Aunt Vera is feeling strong enough to speak
    to a group of women at the NWP headquarters.
        They seat her in the most comfortable chair,
            bring her tea and sweet biscuits. When she has
                eaten what she can, everyone gathers around
            to listen to her stories. I'm puzzled—I know she
        refused the food the guards gave her—but was
    there more to it than that? (Papa: *It could get worse.*)
I've thought hard, and I have not been able to invent
    the details. *First, they put me in the psychiatric ward,*
        Aunt Vera says. *A psychologist interviewed me*
            and pronounced me sane—which was, remarkably,
                the truth, even after I had spent a week in a
            rat-infested prison cell, on a urine-soaked mattress,
        in total isolation. Once they saw that I would not
    give up my hunger strike, they started the force-feeding.
It has nothing to do with nourishment,
    everything to do with power and control.
        Four of us agreed we would not eat. No one
            cared if we died of starvation; their only
                concern was stopping all women from picketing.
            To do that, they would have to break our will,
        and in that, I am happy to report, they did not
succeed. (Am I the only one who doesn't

know what "force-feeding" means? How is it possible
　　　to force someone to open her mouth, and then to swallow,
　　　　　if she refuses to do so?) *Four people—two women and two*
　　　　　　　men—held my arms and legs, Aunt Vera continues,
　　　　　　　　　so I could not move. A fifth tried to open my mouth;
　　　　　　　when I clamped it shut, he pushed something
　　　　　like a shoehorn between my teeth to pry it open.
　　　He forced a tube down my throat into my stomach
and poured food through a funnel into the tube.
　　　They called it "food" though it could have been
　　　　　anything—raw eggs, I believe, probably mixed
　　　　　　　with milk. I couldn't taste it, and I couldn't
　　　　　　　　　keep it down. They did this to the four of us
　　　　　　　three times a day. We could hear one another
　　　　　vomiting, but were not allowed any conversation.
　　　They released me, I'm convinced, not
out of compassion, or morality, but only
　　　because they knew that if I died in prison,
　　　　　they'd have a thousand picketers
　　　　　　　from all around the country on their hands.
　　　　　　　　　A quiet fury gathers in the room. *Vera,*
　　　　　　　Mrs. Ellis says, *women—and some men—*
　　　　　from all around the country are on their way
　　　to Washington right now. We're marching
to protest this kind of treatment, and to continue
　　　our demand for freedom. Tomorrow afternoon,
　　　　　you will be cheered to know, we'll be
　　　　　　　at least one thousand strong.

How Close Can I Go?
Emma

Hands on her hips, Mother stands firm, blocking
the doorway. *I don't want you going over there, Emma.*
Grace is quarantined for up to two weeks. Only her mother
and Dr. Brower (not her father, not Ollie) are allowed in her room.
I understand how my mother feels: I'm all she has left. She can't bear
the thought of losing another child. But that's almost the same way I feel
about Grace. *How close can I go?* I ask. Mother knits her brows. *Don't cross
the creek, Emma. Mrs. Jones died last night. They've closed the school.* This moss-
covered rock by the water is as close as I can be to Grace; I'm trying to heal
her from here with these simple songs I sing. I don't know if she can hear
them; it may be too cold to open her window. Muriel will be home soon.
She doesn't know that now it's her sister who's sick, and her brother
trying his best to hold things together. I'd planned dinner and a
"Welcome Home" party. Now, instead, I sit alone, rocking.

One Thousand Women
Muriel

One thousand women, representing
    every corner of the country, march together
        to the White House, wearing white, with
            gold-and-purple sashes, carrying our banners:
                THE TIME HAS COME TO CONQUER
            OR SUBMIT. THERE CAN BE BUT ONE CHOICE.
        WE HAVE MADE IT. I stand a little taller
and walk on. TO ASK FREEDOM
FOR WOMEN IS NOT A CRIME. SUFFRAGE PRISONERS
SHOULD NOT BE TREATED AS CRIMINALS.
        (A man holds one side of that one.) Aunt Vera
           stands up at a podium, the crowd quiets,
               and she speaks. *They've tried to silence us*
           by every means they know of—our voices
        are still strong. They've tried to hold us
    in their prison cells—our spirit
is stronger than their bars. They've tried
    to force food down our throats—we have not
        accepted it, any more than we accept
           the old, worn-out idea that women are
               the weaker sex. The crowd erupts in cheers.
        They don't have enough prison cells
    to hold us. Their words are not true enough
    to silence us. We are their mothers, sisters,

daughters—here today, one thousand

women strong—our voices will be heard.

President Wilson drives by but doesn't stop,

or even pause to look our way! What is he

afraid of? Will he crack a window open

in the White House and listen like a little boy

when he thinks no one is watching?

Aunt Vera finishes her speech and steps down

from the podium. She finds me in the crowd.

She's still thin, but radiant with joy reflected

to and from these women—and I'm

included, right here at the center.

I'm strong enough, she says, *to travel home.*

(It's time to get back on the train already?)

But, she adds, *I won't be going.* (Why not?)

While I was in prison, my boss sent word

that he's replaced me. (She lost her job!)

Don't worry, she assures me. *I have savings,*

and it won't be hard to find work

when I get back. But I've decided to stay here

in Washington, at least until all the suffrage

prisoners are released. Victory is so close

we can almost touch it! But there's hard work

ahead of us—I'm needed here now, Muriel.

I'm sorry you came all this way for nothing.

I look out at the crowd—today I'm one small part

of something big. *No, Aunt Vera, not for nothing,*

I reply. I straighten out my sash, link arms with her

and Ruby, and the three of us walk forward.

Strangers Together
Muriel

Swing low, sweet chariot, comin' for to carry
me home, a mother in the seat behind me sings
to her baby. The baby cries, then quiets
as the train rocks us, strangers together,
our voices softening as night comes on.
The city noises fade away, and echoes of the
past two weeks collide: young boys selling papers,
Aunt Vera's speech, Ruby's gentle Danish accent
as she speaks to the children in her kindergarten class,
or to me—her parting words: *Come back and teach with me.*
You're good with children, Muriel. I think of Joey,
then doze off and dream of Grace, stretching
out her hand: *When will Muriel come back?*
Emma sings, *I looked over Jordan, and what*
did I see, comin' for to carry me home?
A band of angels, comin' after me, comin' for
to carry me home. But when I wake up, it's not Emma singing;
it's the mother behind me, trying to soothe her baby.
I turn around and offer: *Shall I hold her awhile*
so you can get a little rest? She looks me over:
If she'll let you, that would be kind.
Her name is Viola Irene. I take the baby
in my arms, awkwardly at first, but her hair
has the same sweet smell I remember

from holding Grace when she was a baby,

    and it all comes back. I rock Viola; she smiles

        up at me, making little gurgle sounds—she wants

            to have a conversation. When she falls asleep at last,

                and I return her to her mother, the train

            is quiet, except for someone snoring two seats back.

        I sleep again, a deep sleep without dreaming,

    and wake to a familiar smell: we must have

passed a skunk—not the strong smell

    when their spray gets on your clothes,

        just a soft reminder that I'm nearing home.

Probably . . . If
Ollie

Toss me an onion, Ollie. Pa is trying to cook
while Ma spends all her time taking care of Grace,
who hasn't kept food down for three days. This morning
Dr. Brower came over to see her. *She'll probably live if she
makes it through one more night,* he told us. Every hour, Ma
sends me to the creek—at least I can do *something*—for fresh,
clear water to bathe Grace in order to bring her fever down. I
hear music. Emma? Sitting on a rock beside the creek as she
mends a jacket. Wrapped up in a blanket, singing. Why? It
takes me a minute to realize Emma's here because we've
locked her out. I shouldn't get close, but when she calls
to me, *Ollie! How is she?* I do. She manages a small
smile. *Emma,* I say, *we could lose Grace.* The
loss of my arm is nothing, next to this.

Tell Me About Your Trip
Muriel

Oh, I'm glad you're home, Muriel. Emma hugs me hard
    and we walk to the buggy. Why has she come
        to meet me, instead of Mama or Papa? I'm surprised
            Grace didn't beg to come along. *Emma,* I ask, *how
                is Ollie?* She gives me a quick glance. *Ollie
                is getting better. But . . .* She hesitates, then says,
            Tell me about your trip. Where can I begin?
        *Oh, Emma, I feel like a completely different person
than I was when I left! You should see Washington!
    You can walk down long streets of great mansions!
        But then—just a few blocks away, people live in tiny
            rooms without heat, whole families in one room.
                Some people wearing fur coats and fancy hats
                walk right by children with no coats at all
            as if they don't even see them. Oh, speaking of hats,
    look at this one that I found for Mama. I can't wait
to show it to Grace—she will love these ostrich feathers!*
    Emma clears her throat, but doesn't speak. I go on.
        *I got you and Ollie presents, too, Emma—shall I show you
                now, or wait till we get home? Never mind, I'll wait—
                    they're buried at the bottom of my suitcase.
            And I bought Grace a book,* Anne of Green Gables.
        *But I don't want to sound like all I did
    was shop for presents. I saw the headquarters of the*

National Woman's Party. I stood on a picket line,
    and a tall man hit me with a plank
        because I called him a lazy coward, which he was.
            I still have a small lump on my forehead, but at first
                it was bigger than a goose egg! Ruby—a girl
                I met—said there are some decent men in Washington,
        the same as anywhere, but I didn't meet many of them.
    I met a lot of smart women, though. Ruby teaches
kindergarten—she said I should go back
    someday and teach there because I'm good with children.
        If it weren't for her kindergarten, the children in her class
            would have to go to factories all day with their mothers,
                and a lot of them are put to work, even little ones.
            Some people in Congress are trying to pass child labor laws,
        which I think would be a good idea, don't you? Wait . . .
    Emma . . . you missed the turn to our house.
I guess I'm talking so much you forgot
    where you're going! Emma reins in the horses
        and turns to look at me. She looks tired. Sad?
            I didn't forget, she says. *Your parents asked me*
                to bring you to our house tonight. I wait for her
                to explain, but she goes on in silence, letting the horses
        trot toward her house, not mine. *Emma, what is it?*
    Is something wrong? She has tears in her eyes!
Yes, Muriel, something is very wrong.
    There's Ollie, filling a pail with water from the creek;
        he seems okay—I look more closely—
            has his wound flared up? Emma
                wipes her nose, brushes away tears.
            It's not Ollie, Muriel. It's Grace.

I See That, Too
Emma

Muriel takes a good, hard look at me. The fear
in my eyes must answer the question she doesn't dare
ask. She jumps to the ground, lifts her skirt, and runs. Before
anyone can stop her, she's across Crabapple Creek and halfway
home. Later, when Father takes her suitcase over, they don't invite
him in. *Ollie came to the buggy to meet me,* he says when he gets back.
Grace is still alive. Mother makes them a pot of soup and a loaf of bread.
I can take it over, I offer. Mother draws a deep breath. *No, I'll go instead.*
Father looks up at her, says, *Yes, that's good.* Then, *Ollie doesn't let the lack
of an arm stop him from much, does he?* I see that, too. Late last night
when he heard me singing to Grace, he came out to the creek to say,
I like your singing, Emma, but . . . Grace can't hear you anymore.
I reached out to hold him. *No,* he said, *Please stay where
you are.* Ollie—as always, so thoughtful. So dear.

Lake of Shining Waters
Muriel

"Good night, dear Lake of Shining Waters.
I always say good night to the things I love
just as I would to people. I think they like it.
That water looks as if it was smiling at me."
    I bought *Anne of Green Gables* for Grace,
and I intend to read every word of it to her.
When she gets better, she can read it all again.
I say *when,* not *if.* I refuse to consider *if.*
Reading the story keeps me from shouting at her:
Listen here, Grace, you open your eyes right now.
Mrs. Norman went to the trouble to make this soup.
She even brought it over here herself! You'd better
wake up and eat it. Quit acting like this, do you
understand me? Mama and Papa and Dr. Brower told me
to stay out of Grace's room, but—like Frank and Ollie
going to war—I'm old enough to decide for myself
what I'll risk, and who I'll risk it for, and why.
If I can stand up to that stupid man
who hit me with a board, if I can hold a banner
for the president to read, and—I'm not exactly sure
what this has to do with anything—if I can
give away an apple and a shoelace when someone
needs them, and sing a lullaby to Viola Irene,
I'm not going to let this flu prevent me

from loving my own sister! When Mama saw
    that I would not be stopped, she said, *Well, then,*
        maybe I'll sleep a bit—just an hour or so.
            Wake me if there is any change.
                There is no change—Grace is burning up;
            her breath goes in and out. She has been sleeping
        for two days, and all our love can't wake her.

Tipperary
  Ollie

Dread is thick as mud in our house, as Emma's
song washes over us, a stream of cool water. Muriel is
staying up all night, reading that book to Grace. (Does she
think Grace is listening?) For the first time all week, Pa and Ma
are both asleep. *Open the window a little wider, Muriel,* I suggest.
I'm going to the creek for water. She probably guesses that, though I
will get water for her to cool Grace, I'm going to see Emma. *Are you
still sitting on this rock in the dark?* I ask. *Have you been out here all this
time, huddled in your blanket?* She nods. I shake my head. *I bet even the
war wouldn't scare you like it scares the fellows over there.* I give her a
drink from the creek. She accepts it, takes a small sip, and says, *I'm
praying as I sing, Ollie.* That's good. *But,* I ask, *is there anything
wrong with praying a cheerful song?* She smiles: *Tipperary?*
Red streaks the sky as we sing: *It's a long way . . .*

Then What Happened?
Muriel

Then what happened?
    I've walked to the window to listen
        to Ollie and Emma singing together
            and at first I don't believe my ears—
                I turn to look—I'm not imagining things—
            that question came out of Grace!
    I stopped reading for a minute,
  turned away, and she opened her eyes to ask
what happened next! *I don't know, Grace,*
  I'm reading it for the first time myself.
      Mama said to wake her if there was any change,
          but Grace insists, *Keep reading, Muriel.*
             I think Anne really does like Gilbert, don't you?
      She keeps her eyes open, and I go on, as if
    reading is breathing, and by reading I can
  keep my sister breathing. *"Then, just as she thought*
she really could not endure the ache in her arms and wrists
  another moment, Gilbert Blythe came rowing under the bridge . . ."
      Grace actually grins! *See, I told you, Muriel!*
        Ollie's clear baritone and Emma's alto
            come to me across the early morning air:
        We didn't know (Ollie's voice)
    the way to tickle Mary (soft laughter),
  but we learned how, over there.

Let's Climb Cobb Hill
Emma

Ollie suggests, *Let's climb Cobb Hill*
to watch the sunrise. We don't talk while we climb
the narrow path through the trees. When we reach the top,
we sit down on a fallen log and Ollie says, *Emma, I've been trying*
to find a way to tell you something important, and there's no fancy way
of saying it. Ollie has never been fancy with words; that's fine—I wait
for him to find the solid, plain words he is looking for. He stares down
at his feet, looks up at me, takes a deep breath. Tears flood his brown
eyes. He blinks them back. *I'm sorry about Frank,* he says. A great
heaviness rises up, drapes itself around us. Ollie goes on: *All day*
when I was thinking about Grace, I would picture you crying
for your brother when I was over there . . . I can't stop
feeling guilty. I wasn't much of a soldier—I'm
sorry. (For what?) *I couldn't learn to kill.*

In the Doorway
Muriel

" 'Dear old world,' she murmured, 'you are very lovely,
    and I am glad to be alive in you.' " I can barely keep
        my eyes open, but Grace won't let me stop reading
           until we get to the end. Mama opens the door
             and sees Grace sitting up, eyes bright,
           attentive to the story. She catches her breath,
        comes in, and rests her hand on Grace's forehead,
    staring at her like she did eight years ago,
that August afternoon when Grace was born.
    A warm breeze blew through the house that day—
        as a fresh, cool wind blows now. Grace is smiling!
           Mama stands behind her, brushing her hair,
             and I read the last page of the book:
             " 'God's in his heaven, all's right with the world,'
        whispered Anne softly." I close the book and then
    I close my eyes. It's been two days since I've slept,
apart from a few hours on the train.
    Get some sleep now, Muriel, says Mama.
        Thank you, God, she breathes. *Thank you, Muriel,*
        says Papa as I pass him in the doorway.

I Had My Rifle, Loaded
Ollie

Crown him Lord of all, Emma sings through a
haze of tears, a triumphant song of quiet strength.
We're standing together by the water. I have come to tell her
Grace got up and ate an egg; after Emma weeps and sings, we stay
to talk. *Grace is like a sister to me,* Emma says. Then she listens as I
tell her about the war; like Muriel, she doesn't ask too many questions.
My memory of it clears in patches, thick fog rising off a field. *But Emma,*
why couldn't I shoot him? That bothers me. I had my rifle, loaded with a
shell—after all my training, I couldn't kill a man. She thinks about it.
You have been tenderhearted as long as I've known you. It's not my
place to try to read your mind—but I don't think it was only
fear. She dips her fingers in the creek, then lets them
graze my cheeks, trying to smooth away my
frown. *Let love wash the war away.*

A Small, Cold Stone
Muriel

You've been asleep for thirteen hours, Mama tells me.
    I've been dreaming I was on a train, holding
        a baby, singing "It's a Long Way to Tipperary."
            (What a funny song to sing to a baby.) I dreamed
                a soldier came and took the baby from me;
            I'll bring her right back, he said, but he
    got off the train and it went on without them,
    moving too fast for me to follow and get the baby back.
I blink, trying to remember both the dream
    and what has happened since I got home.
        Was the train in the dream going to Washington?
            Who was sitting with me—Ruby? Was the baby
                hers? No . . . someone's little sister . . . Oh!
            Grace . . . *How is she?* I ask. Mama looks tired,
    but she smiles. *Grace will be fine, Muriel.*
Dr. Brower is as surprised as we are.
Three of his patients have died this week—they've canceled
the dance on Saturday, and won't have school
    for at least another week, to keep the flu from spreading.
        Who is that, whistling at the door? Ollie
            comes in, so happy I hardly recognize him.
        I thought you'd never wake up, Muriel!
    Grace is going to be okay! She is *okay! And*
Emma says you brought presents from Washington.

I turn to find my suitcase—it's true, I do have gifts
            for everyone—but something catches at the edge
                        of my attention: a small, cold stone sinking
                                    into a depth I can't quite see.
                                                "Emma says . . ." said Ollie? She told him
                                    what I told her, and he is telling me
                        what she told him. Something here
            has shifted while I've been away.

With Our Three Arms
Emma

Ollie gently mentions Frank: *I hate to see you cry*
about your brother. I'll try to do things he would have done
for you. The kindness in his eyes and voice loosens a tight place
deep inside me, releasing an ache I've been trying not to feel. Instead
of simply saying "Thank you," I start to tremble, my shoulders shake,
and I can't stop myself from crying. Ollie, startled, steps back. *I'm sorry,*
Emma. Of course no one can take Frank's place. I know I could never . . .
His arm drops to his side. I nod my head: *It's okay.* All the tears I've ever
kept myself from crying seem to be falling now, torrential. *Don't worry,*
Emma, I don't mean . . . I want . . . I put my finger to his lips to make
him stop apologizing. He leans down to kiss my forehead . . .
and then somehow, with our three arms, we embrace.
I whisper, *You're not my brother, Ollie*—I find one
clear smile—*and I don't want you to try.*

Nothing in the World
Muriel

It's true, Muriel. I saw them, Grace confides.
They didn't see me, though—Emma might think
I'm still sick. I'm sure Ollie has told Emma
that Grace is out of bed, but it's true that Grace
can be so quiet you don't know she's there.
Why shouldn't I believe her? Ollie and Emma,
hugging and kissing—I'm not surprised.
Emma has always had a soft spot in her heart
for Ollie, though he has never quite believed it.
Two people I care for, together now—I'm . . .
happy for them. *What's wrong, Muriel?* Grace's question
catches me off guard. I'm on the edge of tears—
I don't know how to answer. *Nothing,*
Grace, nothing in the world is wrong.
Is that closer to the truth than I admit?
Nothing. Is that what will be left for me, if
Emma and Ollie are to be a pair? At home, we were
always Frank and Emma, Muriel and Ollie.
At school, it was Frank and Ollie,
Muriel and Emma. If Frank is gone, and now
it's Emma matched with Ollie, where
does that leave me? With no one.
Nothing. Nothing in the world.

Worth Knowing
Ollie

Clever words and witty conversation are not
how I make friends. Still, I never dreamed that being
nice could be enough to get a girl to notice me. All these years,
I haven't dared to hope for Emma's love. And now, the past two days,
old tunes come whistling back to me from who knows where; it's like an
"all clear" in my mind. *Yankee Doodle went to town, a-riding on his pony,
stuck a feather in his cap and called it macaroni.* Macaroni? Something
struck me this morning while I was whistling that song: What did he
call macaroni, anyhow—the feather, the cap, or the pony? It's not a
bold original thought, no one has to tell me, but it stopped me in
my tracks to realize: it's the first time, since that bullet took a
slice out of my shoulder, I've had such cheerful thoughts.
Wow—that's a fact worth knowing. Something can
sever an arm without destroying your brain.

A Quick Nod
Muriel

Oh—you shouldn't have! Most people,
　　when they say that, make it sound like *thank you,*
　　　　but when Mama says it, I always feel I've done
　　　　　　something wrong. Spent too much money,
　　　　　　　　made a careless purchase, chosen a color
　　　　　　　　that is not quite right. *But Mama,* I argue, *it looks nice*
　　　　　　on you—I saw lots of women in Washington, D.C.,
　　　　wearing hats like this one. She gives me a quick glance
(am I putting on airs?), longing—I can see it—
　　not exactly for the hat itself, but to be the kind of
　　　　person who could wear it. *I don't know, girls . . .*
　　　　　　(Is Grace going to cry?) Mama tilts her head
　　　　　　　　and looks at me—a peculiar mix of love and
　　　　　　　　hard appraisal, with a touch of guilty vanity
　　　　　　tossed in. Grace grabs her hand—Mama can't stop
　　　　herself from smiling. She gives a quick nod of
acceptance. *Thank you, Grace, it's lovely.*
　　Thank you, Muriel, she says.

I Can See Myself
Emma

Corn, potatoes, butternut squash. A woodchuck
waddles through the garden. A V of geese flies overhead.
I've always loved this time of year, when all the work we've done
comes back to feed us. We put up ten jars of pickles, fifty pints of beans,
sixty-five quarts of applesauce. Now I see Ollie, crossing the creek, carrying
something to our house. *Look, Emma,* he says, *here's the first fish I've caught
since I've been home!* Just last week, we were all afraid that Grace might die,
and now she (and everyone else, too) is brimming over with exuberant life. I
was thinking that if Muriel ever takes another trip to Washington, I ought
to go along—but it's not likely. I can see myself staying here, marrying
Ollie someday. I know Muriel is restless. She thinks marriage means
we'd be hemming ourselves in. Mother calls her plucky. But one
life can't be less full than another; making sure everyone is fed
and clothed and cared for—that also takes a kind of pluck.

Bluebird Stitched in Such Detail

December 1917

We Have Reason to Believe
Muriel

Aunt Vera sends me a small parcel—
    a box of suffrage pins and fliers, a program
        from a speech she heard, along with a three-page
            letter, all about her work. *I'm fully recovered,*
                and all the prisoners have been released,
            but I've decided to stay here and see this through.
        A vote comes up in Congress on January 10th.
    We have reason to believe the president
will offer his support this time! Everyone here sends
greetings to you, Muriel, asking when you
        will return. Ruby asked me to enclose her letter—
            consider what she asks of you. We need
                all hands on deck these coming weeks,
            and I would love to see you be a part
    of what could be a historic time for women.
Whatever you decide—thank you for coming
in November. Your presence helped me
    more than I can say. Give my love
        to everyone in Michigan. With fond affection
            (and power to women everywhere!),
                Aunt Vera.

My Friend Miss Muriel
Muriel

Dear Muriel, Ruby writes, *I'm glad to hear*
      you make it safely home, and that your sister
         is recover from her flu. I won't beat the bush—
            is that how you say it? I hope you
                  think about come back to Washington.
            She says they need an assistant kindergarten
        teacher, and if I want the job, it's mine! *Remember*
Joey, the little boy who not could tie his shoes?
Now, every time he tie them, he say, "My friend
     Miss Muriel teach me how." I haven't told Mama
        much about my trip yet, and she's full of questions:
           Who is Ruby? How did you meet her?
               Where does she live? Does Vera know her?
           I put the letter in my pocket while I take my time
        to think this through. In the kitchen, making rolls
    with Grace and Mama, I let my thoughts go back and forth
from here (What if Grace gets sick again, and I'm not here
    to help?) to Washington (Ruby says I would be paid
        enough to support myself if I live where she lives—
           a room is vacant now, and I could have it).
             Ollie/Joey. Ruby/Emma. Mama and Papa/
        Aunt Vera and the other suffrage women.
     Grace—nothing in Washington comes close
    to balancing how I'd miss Grace. I go out to feed the hens,
scattering these thoughts as I scatter corn, then climb

Cobb Hill to see if any answers come to me.
        I look out over our two farms—
                there's Mr. Norman coming home from work,
                        stopping at the clothesline to kiss Mrs. Norman
                and help her hang the sheet she's struggling with.
        I think about Grace—I left her sitting
by the window reading *Anne of Green Gables*
for the third time. Mama came in to feel her forehead,
        as if to reassure herself: *Thank God, yes,*
                Grace is still here, Grace is fine. I see Papa trying
                        to repair the windmill by himself. Where is Ollie?
                        Where, come to think of it, is Emma? I start
                back down the hill—maybe I can help Papa
        fix the windmill. I pass by Grace's playhouse,
recalling that day last June, when Ollie
(with both arms) worked so hard to finish it.
Grace seemed so much younger then,
        jumping up and down as she watched him work.
                Wait . . . what do I hear? Someone
                        in the playhouse—not Grace—
                two voices—*Shhh . . . she'll hear us.*
        Soft whisper—*We shouldn't . . .*
I hurry on; I don't want to hear more.
I am "she," I'm sure of it.
Ollie and Emma are "we."
        This is how it is, how it will be
                from now on—their new forever.
                        I start composing letters in my mind:
                Dear Ruby, I will take the job.
                Dear Aunt Vera, Count me in.

It Also Happened to Us
Ollie

Tie his shoes? Muriel is leaving home because she taught
a child in Washington to tie his shoes? I don't understand. Aren't
there plenty of children around here that she could teach? Pa and Ma
are determined not to tell her what to do: *It's up to you. We'll miss you,
but you're old enough to decide for yourself. If you've made up your mind,
we won't try to change it.* Pa is very quiet. Ma is thinking hard. I heard her
crying after Muriel went to bed. She looks tired. Maybe she's lonely. I'm
trying to recall how it was before—Mrs. Norman came over all the time.
She was here almost every day, before the war, I remind Emma. *That's
what you don't understand,* Emma answers. *We've changed, too. The
war happened to you over in France, but it also happened to us
here at home.* She holds my hand. I think about that. *Yes, I*
say, *but now maybe it's time for us to make some blackberry
pie and fried chicken! Get together for a little music.*

Blackberry-Apple Cobbler
Muriel

It won't be easy, leaving home;
    Ollie sounds so mournful when he
        talks about it, I'll never tell him my decision
            has anything to do with him. In truth, it doesn't;
                hearing him and Emma whispering together
                in the playhouse was just the nudge I needed
            to make me go out looking for whatever happiness
    will be my own. I promise Grace, *I'll come home*
as often as I can. And when you're old enough
    to take the train, you can come and visit me.
        Emma hears our conversation and offers
            to come to Washington on the train with Grace.
                Ollie and Emma have accomplished what
                Mama, Grace, and I could not: the two of them
            have brought our families together, almost
    like we were before Frank and Ollie went to war.
Ollie invited Mrs. Norman over, so sweetly, Emma told me,
    that she could not refuse, and Mr. Norman
        said of course they'd come: *We have a lot to celebrate.*
            Here they come now, crossing Crabapple Creek,
                Mrs. Norman carrying her blackberry-apple
            cobbler—I've been missing that these past few months.
    Why is Mr. Norman carrying Frank's banjo?
Grace, he says when they arrive, *you've said*

you'd like to learn to play an instrument.

This was Frank's—we gave it to him when he

was not much older than you are. Now

we're giving it to you. Mama's hand

goes to her mouth—she glances up—

Mrs. Norman gives a brief nod

and they both look at Grace, who simply answers,

Thank you, Mr. Norman. Will you teach me

how to play it? Mr. Norman smiles.

Yes, he says. *My father's uncle taught him,*

he taught me, I taught Fr—

I taught . . . my boy . . .

I'd be happy to teach you.

One Hand, Drying
Emma

Muriel and I are in the kitchen with our mothers, frying
chicken, slicing sweet potatoes. Mrs. Jorgensen lays out her best blue
tablecloth, the one she brought from the old country. As we set the table
for eight instead of nine, we pause, but no one says Frank's name out loud.
The men come in together—they have managed to repair the windmill. I pay
attention, watching how Ollie's mother helps him when he needs it, without
embarrassing him. She cuts his food into bite-size pieces before she brings
it to the table and she moves his spoon to the left side of his plate. Things
I might not have noticed if . . . (Does Muriel know I'm thinking about
marrying her brother?) He glances over at me. He's found a way
to wash his hand and dry it. Is he showing off a bit, proud
of the muscle in his arm? (*Look, Emma, I'm capable.*
I can carry two chairs in one hand.) Inviting me to
witness his accomplishment: one hand, drying.

Bluebird Stitched in Such Detail
Muriel

After supper, Mr. Norman teaches Grace
     to play Frank's banjo—she learns quickly. Emma
          sits beside Ollie, humming the tune Grace plays.
               Mama and Papa are outside looking at the windmill
                    and I'm standing by myself at the window.
               Mrs. Norman studies me. She's holding
          something white—clean, ironed, neatly folded.
Muriel? she says, careful not to interrupt my thoughts.
I have something for you. She unfolds the pillowcase
     she's been embroidering all these weeks—thousands
          of tiny stitches, daisies and roses and butterflies,
               and in one corner, a bluebird stitched in such detail
                    it looks like it will fly right off the cloth into the sky.
               It's something I'd expect her to give Emma
          as a wedding gift—why is she giving it to me?
     I know the answer without asking: she's been stitching
all her dreams for Frank, trying to hold them steady—
     no doubt I'm part of them. She holds it out to me;
          I put my hands under hers and let the pillowcase
               drape both our arms. Then I'm crying,
                    we both are, our tears watering the garden
               she has made. *Thank you,* I say,
          and she says, *Those are lucky children,*
waiting for you in Washington.

The Scent of Soap
Ollie

Slings. Bandages. Red cross and white cap.

Smell of antiseptic. Squeaking wheel on the medic's cart.

Cold sweat—I wake up. No, I'm not over there—then where am I?

I must be home. Yes, here in my childhood room. (I hope I didn't scream.)

Alone, dark night. But yes, home. I've been dreaming, remembering the war . . .

yet not only the war. Something new . . . like clean sheets, fresh off the clothesline,

sweet. Maybe the scent of soap? Lilac soap. And Emma's whisper. Oh! I remember.

Meet me at midnight in Grace's playhouse, Ollie. I was so sure I wouldn't fall asleep! I

get up (everyone else seems to be sleeping) and meet Emma as we planned. I take

a stone I've polished, and offer it. *It's beautiful,* she says. Then she mentions

my missing arm. She says, *Let me see it.* The stump of it? *No!* I say. I've

told her it is hideous. She touches it through my shirt. I'm adamant.

Tell me why not, Ollie. It's one part of—who I love. So I show her.

Wings of a butterfly could not be as gentle as Emma's touch.

I Step onto the Train

January 1918

Now, in the Distance
Muriel

I could still change my mind.
    Until I'm actually on the train—I hear it now
        in the distance—I could turn to Mama
            (wearing her new hat) and Papa, each holding
                one of Grace's hands. I could turn to Emma—
        and to Ollie, carrying my suitcase with such
    a natural rhythm anyone would think he's had
only one arm since he was born. I could turn
to Mrs. Norman, standing at Mr. Norman's side, his hand
    resting on her shoulder. I could turn to all of them
        and say, *I'm not going after all. I'm staying here.*
            There would be no shame in that. My place
                here could still be opened in all the ways
        it has begun to close. I know this
    as the train approaches, as the whistle drowns
all necessity and possibility of saying any of it.
The train comes to a stop where we are standing,
    and Ollie swings my suitcase up onto the train
        as the conductor yells his *All aboard!*
            I step onto the train and turn to wave goodbye,
                then pick up my suitcase and go to find my place.

Epilogue

Muriel arrived in Washington, D.C., in time to be a part of the final push for woman suffrage. A combination of courage, determination, and careful strategy helped the suffragists win the support of President Woodrow Wilson on January 9, 1918; the next day, the House of Representatives passed the Nineteenth Amendment to the U.S. Constitution. The women, and the men who supported them, continued to work until, on August 26, 1920, the Amendment was signed into law, granting women the right to vote.

Like Muriel, and the other characters in *Crossing Stones*, Frank Norman is fictional, but his war experience reflects that of the more than eight million people who were killed in battle in World War I. By the time the war ended on November 11, 1918, over sixty-five million people throughout the world had fought in it, and total casualties (including deaths, wounded, and prisoners of war or missing in action) added up to over thirty-seven million.

In addition to the war itself, a deadly influenza epidemic spread through the battlefields, killing millions, and when the soldiers returned home, many of them carried it back to their families and communities. The flu spread worldwide, killing between twenty and forty million people in 1918 and 1919.

I considered continuing my story until Muriel casts her first ballot. But when I look closely at this image—a ballot in a woman's hand—I see that the hand is not Muriel's, or not only hers. It is my grandmother's hand, voting in her first election when my mother was three years old; my mother's hand, my aunts' hands, my sisters' and nieces', my own—and now, your sister's, your daughter's, your own.

So I leave them here: Ollie and Emma in the circle of their new love, and Muriel moving with confidence toward all that she will accomplish in her life as a happily unmarried woman.

Notes on the Form

Acknowledgments

Notes on the Form

I've created a formal structure to give the sense of stepping from stone to stone across a flowing creek. I think of this kind of writing as painting with words, a process involving hands, eyes, ears, thought, and emotion, all simultaneously working together.

The relatively free style of Muriel's poems represents the creek flowing over the stones as it pushes against its banks. Ollie's and Emma's poems represent the stones. I "painted" them to look round and smooth, each with a slightly different shape, like real stones. They are "cupped-hand sonnets," fourteen-line poems in which the first line rhymes with the last line, the second line rhymes with the second-to-last, and so on, so that the seventh and eighth lines rhyme with each other at the poem's center. In Ollie's poems the rhymes are the beginning words of each line, and in Emma's poems they are the end words.

To give the sense of stepping from one stone to the next, I have used the middle rhyme of one sonnet as the outside rhyme of the next. You will see that the seventh and eighth lines of each of Emma's poems rhyme with the first and last lines of Ollie's next poem, and the seventh and eighth lines of Ollie's poems rhyme with the first and last lines of Emma's next poem. If you have trouble finding these rhymes, remember to look on the left side of Ollie's poems, and on the right side of Emma's.

Acknowledgments

I thank Frances Foster for her constant faith, encouragement, and editorial skill, and everyone at Farrar, Straus and Giroux for all they do, with special thanks to Lisa Graff.

Don Mager worked out the cupped-hand sonnet form and shared it with me. Jonas Albertsen, my father's Danish cousin, suggested Ruby's Danish name and helped me with her language. I thank them.

Thanks to the Indiana chapter of the Society of Children's Book Writers and Illustrators, especially the Fort Wayne group, and many trusted friends and faithful readers.

The time in which *Crossing Stones* takes place is a fascinating period of history. Librarians, novelists, psychologists, historians, film-makers, letter writers, and family archivists all give us access to the past, and I am grateful. A visit to the Hull House Museum in Chicago was especially helpful.

I thank those who understand the history and importance of the progressive movement and work to continue its forward momentum. Among the many people whose work inspires me are John and Beth Murphy Beams, Ann Colbert, Claire Ewart and Tom Herr, the Liuzzi family, Omowale-Ketu and Clydia Oladuwa, Ron and Suzanne Scollon, Sox Sperry and Lisa Tsetse, and Ralph Salisbury and Ingrid Wendt.

I thank my family—the ancestors who lived with love and courage through the times I am imagining, especially my parents (my mother was born a week before this story begins and lived to admire Richard Tuschman's beautiful jacket artwork); my brothers and sisters, their husbands, wives, children, and grandchildren; and my husband's family. Special love and thanks to my son, Lloyd, and his wife, Penny; their children, Cameron and Jordan; and my son, Glen.

As always, I am immensely grateful to my husband, Chad Thompson, beside me and within this book in countless ways.